'You look less like a born and bred school-marm than you did this morning.'

Cliff's gaze rested on her loose hair that had a tendency to be full and wayward when unconfined.

A tinge of colour stole into Sarah's cheeks but she forced herself to say coolly, 'Flattery will get you nowhere, Mr Wyatt. I adjusted to not being a raving beauty years ago.'

Dear Reader

It's the time of year when nights are long and cold, and there's nothing better than relaxing with a Mills & Boon story! To help you banish those winter blues, we've got some real treats in store for you this month. Enjoy the first book in our exciting new LOVE LETTERS series, or forget the weather outside and lose yourself in one of our exotic locations. It's almost as good as a real winter holiday!

The Editor

Lindsay Armstrong was born in South Africa but now lives in Australia with her New Zealand-born husband and their five children. They have lived in nearly every state of Australia and tried their hand at some unusual, for them, occupations, such as farming and horse-training—all grist to the mill for a writer! Lindsay started writing romances when their youngest child began school and she was left feeling at a loose end. She is still doing it and loving it.

Recent titles by the same author:

AN UNSUITABLE WIFE
A MASTERFUL MAN

TRIAL BY MARRIAGE

BY
LINDSAY ARMSTRONG

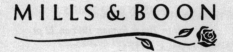

MILLS & BOON LIMITED
ETON HOUSE, 18-24 PARADISE ROAD
RICHMOND, SURREY TW9 1SR

*MILLS & BOON and the Rose Device
are trademarks of the publisher.*

*First published in Great Britain 1994
by Mills & Boon Limited*

© Lindsay Armstrong 1994

*Australian copyright 1994   Philippine copyright 1995
This edition 1995*

ISBN 0 263 78810 5

*Set in Times Roman 10½ on 12 pt.
01-9501-50263 C*

Made and printed in Great Britain

CHAPTER ONE

'How do you do, Ms Sutherland? Sit down, please.'

Sarah Sutherland hesitated briefly and blinked a couple of times. She'd just been introduced to Cliff Wyatt and found the experience a little breathtaking. So she sat in front of the old oak desk, unable to think of anything to say, and waited for him to continue.

He did, after a slight pause, during which she felt as if every detail of her person had been thoroughly scrutinised. He said, directing his gaze back to her rather delicate oval face dominated by a pair of horn-rimmed spectacles, 'As you know I've taken over Edgeleigh Station and, as you've probably divined, a few changes will need to be made. A combination of drought, low beef prices, old-fashioned methods and so on have seen the property run at a loss lately so some economies are required. Therefore, can you give me three good reasons for keeping you on?'

Sarah stared at Cliff Wyatt with widening eyes—he was not sitting as she was now but resting his tall frame negligently against a window-frame behind his chair and he was probably, she thought, still a bit dazedly, the best-looking man she'd seen for years. He had thick, dark hair, dark eyes, good-looking features with a faintly olive skin, a well-cut mouth and the kind of physique that would have done an athlete proud—very wide shoulders, narrow hips, long legs and he had to be at least six feet six.

And second impressions, she realised, reinforced his good looks, because there was an aura about him, in his impeccable yellow Lacoste shirt and beautifully tailored khaki trousers, of raw power combined with sophistication, the aura of a man you would be foolish to tangle with, of intellect, of charm if you were lucky, scorn if you weren't. And there was little charm being directed at her at present, she decided. Rather a businesslike and indifferent manner, as indeed his question had conveyed.

She sat up straighter, remembering that question. 'I can give you a dozen good reasons, Mr Wyatt,' she said tartly, 'plus another recurring dozen or so, but, if you can't *see* the advantage of having a proper school and a resident teacher on a property this size and this remote, I could be wasting my time.'

He raised an eyebrow and murmured, 'Spoken like a true school-marm. Well——' he pulled out the chair and sat down himself '—let's proceed on your assumption that I'm dense and a Philistine. In other words, do enlighten me. But I would just like to state that I'm all for education and my question was not based on an indifference to good schooling.' He picked up a pen, dangled it between his long fingers and regarded her with a sort of pensive arrogance that caused her some more annoyance.

So she said thoughtfully, 'I read somewhere that it's a grave insult to the Philistines to regard them as ignorant, uncultured and unartistic but, since you brought it up in that context and as applied to yourself, all right. The School of the Air does a wonderful job but it's an *alternative* when the proper facilities are not available. In this case, the facilities are already here, thanks to the care and consideration of the previous owners.' She shot him an ironic little look from behind her horn-rimmed glasses and went on evenly, 'I can also guarantee that *all* of my pupils have benefited from my personal tuition, and, if you don't believe me, check with their parents. Of course...' she paused and regarded Cliff Wyatt steadily '... if you can't *afford* me, that's another matter.'

The expression in Cliff Wyatt's fine dark eyes didn't change as he said musingly, 'You're handy with your tongue, I see, Ms Sutherland. I always did believe school-marms were born and not made. Why...' he paused and looked her over consideringly again, taking in her plain white cotton shirt, her jeans and boots, her lack of make-up and any sort of artifice, her glasses, her long chestnut hair worn with a fringe and tied back with a rubber band '... you even look like the kind of spinster that is born so admirably to the vocation. You are, I gather, a confirmed spinster?' he added, looking fleetingly down at the papers in front of him, and continued before she could speak, 'Ah, yes, twenty-six and unmarried, never married and never likely to be, perhaps. No, it doesn't say that here; it's just my intuition,' he said gently as her mouth fell open. 'But you wouldn't be a bad-looking girl if you took some trouble, you know. A bit thin, a bit intense maybe—the two do often go together— but nice skin and hair and——' He stopped unhur-riedly as Sarah rose and slammed a fist on to the desk so that all his papers jumped.

Nor did he look at all perturbed as she said through her teeth, 'How dare you? I should like nothing better than to—punch you in the mouth!'

He smiled for the first time. 'Now that would be interesting but perhaps a little unequal. For one thing,

I don't know about picking you up with one hand but I certainly could with two so I really think we'd be better off to continue trading insults rather than blows. Do you——' he looked at her quizzically '—make a habit of going around offering to beat people up?'

Sarah drew a deep, shaky breath and sat down rather suddenly, as it occurred to her to wonder whether she'd gone mad. 'No,' she said curtly, and breathed deeply again. 'No,' she said again, more collectedly although she was still angry, 'but I must confess that I've never been insulted quite like this before—do *you* make a habit of going around offering verbal abuse to all and sundry in this manner, Mr Wyatt?'

'Not usually,' he replied with a sudden grin and lay back in his chair. 'I do believe the first shot in this little war was yours, however.'

'I hesitate to contradict you,' Sarah retorted, 'but you immediately put me on the defensive by implying that there might be *no* good reason to keep the school going and then uttering offensive remarks about school-marms!'

'That's all?' he murmured, but as she opened her mouth and closed it immediately he went on with only a wicked little glint in his eye, 'As to good reasons or otherwise, may I make a couple of points? There will be no school even to argue about if Edgeleigh goes broke, so I can't afford too many philanthropic gestures and I need to make some rapid decisions as the new owner and employer.' He smiled faintly. 'As an employer it's handy to get to the heart of things as swiftly as possible and that's often done best in a direct, no-nonsense manner. But now that I've met you, Miss Sutherland, and incidentally been told by at least three pairs of parents that you're an excellent teacher and they don't know what they'd do without you, as well as having seen your—impassioned stance on the subject, you may stay. For the time being.'

'Did you . . . did you,' Sarah tried again, 'try to unsettle, not to mention antagonise, all your other employees in your capacity as a direct, no-nonsense employer this morning, Mr Wyatt? Or was it only me?'

'Now why should you imagine I would single you out for special treatment, Miss Sutherland?' he countered.

'Because of an innate aversion to spinsters such as only aggressively, unpleasantly macho men can have?' Sarah suggested with withering scorn.

'Dear me.' Cliff Wyatt sat up and looked at her with lazy amusement. 'I perceive some interesting times ahead of us, Miss Sutherland. It would be funny if we discovered we weren't at cross purposes at all, wouldn't it?'

'I have no idea what you mean.'

'I wonder?' He shrugged. 'In the meantime perhaps I should confine myself to running the place and you to your school. That way we might manage to...limit this conflict before it gets out of hand. I take it you are going to stay?' He looked at her quizzically again.

Sarah bit her lip and tried to stop herself but rarely had her emotions been so turbulent and she heard herself say caustically, 'I guess so but I shall certainly do all in my power to stay out of *your* way.'

'Good.' He stood up. 'You'll have two new pupils, incidentally.'

'Oh?'

'My sister's children. She'll be living here with me for the time being. She and her husband have split up. They're six and seven. Would you care to be introduced now or would you like time to calm down and wrest your thoughts from the frustrations of aggressively, unpleasantly macho men?'

Sarah's lips parted and her eyes sparked dangerously behind her glasses but as she opened her mouth to speak the door flew open and four people entered the study.

'Well, that takes care of that,' Cliff Wyatt murmured. 'Miss Sutherland, may I introduce you to my sister Amy, my niece and nephew, Sally and Ben, and Wendy Wilson? Amy, this is...Sarah, I believe, Sutherland, the schoolteacher.'

The next few minutes were confused but Sarah was conscious of several overriding impressions—that Amy Weston and Wendy Wilson, who was apparently her best friend, were both glossy, beautifully groomed and clothed girls who couldn't have looked more out of place on a cattle station if they'd tried in their designer gear, with their long, painted nails, flimsy sandals and expertly applied make-up. They were also striking contrasts, with Amy being a delicate honey-blonde, about five feet two, while Wendy was dark, taller with a stunning figure and beautiful yet curiously worldly green eyes.

Sally and Ben were both fair and blue-eyed like their mother, but, whereas Sally hung back shyly, Ben caused Sarah to smile inwardly as she recognised all the signs of an energetic, dare-devil, naughty-as-they-come little boy.

And once the rather confused greetings had taken place Amy said, 'Well, thank heavens there's a *school*, but honestly, Cliff, this place is unbelievable! The house is archaic and there are workmen everywhere, and it's so...' She gestured helplessly. 'It's... We might as well be stuck out beyond the black stump! I didn't realise it was this far away, and this *bush*,' she said intensely.

'But I warned you, Amy,' Cliff Wyatt said impatiently. 'Although the house will be finished shortly and there are all sorts of mod cons going in. Besides which you have a housekeeper so you won't really have to lift a finger, little though you're capable of it,' he said drily, and added, 'Tell me this, would you rather have stayed, perhaps *languished* is a better word, alone in Brisbane since you tell me you have no intention of going back to Coorilla?'

Amy disregarded the insults entirely and looked wistful. 'At least I could go shopping in Brisbane. And I've just met the housekeeper, Cliff,' she added with more spirit. 'She...well, I'm lost for words!'

Wendy Wilson stirred. 'She's probably got a heart of gold underneath that mountainous frame and peculiar—er—manner,' she suggested in a husky, oddly sexy voice.

'She has,' Sarah said.

All eyes switched to her and it interested Sarah to note that it was Wendy, not Amy, who drawled, 'You could probably help us out a bit, Miss Sutherland. As you see we rather feel like fish out of water at the moment. Would you mind...helping us to find our feet among the locals a bit?'

'Not at all,' Sarah said although she knew that most of the locals would view both girls with the utmost suspicion, possibly for a good long time. She also started to feel annoyed again because the other girl was assessing her quite openly and contriving to make her feel aware that she was neither groomed nor glossy as well as very much an employee.

'Then that's settled,' Cliff Wyatt said firmly. 'Take 'em away if you wouldn't mind, Miss Sutherland; I have enough to do as it is. Oh, I'd like to check the schoolhouse out, though, and all the facilities you're so proud of...uh, say around four this afternoon? I'll meet you there.' And he turned away and picked up the phone.

'Cliff can be impossible at times,' Amy said disconsolately.

They were in the huge homestead kitchen where Sarah had led them. Edgeleigh homestead was a rather lovely if dilapidated example of Queensland colonial architecture, with spacious, high-ceilinged rooms, deep verandas running around it and a steep green roof. Because she'd become friends with the previous owners, Sarah knew the house well and she was relieved to see that the mod cons Cliff Wyatt had mentioned applied only to bathrooms and the kitchen and that the rest of the house was being restored to its former glory, with fresh paint and repairs being made in character with the style of the period.

'Cliff is in the position of being able to do as he likes,' Wendy Wilson said a shade drily. 'And you have to admit you'd have been miserable on your own in Brisbane, darling.'

'I suppose so.' Tears sparkled momentarily on Amy's lashes then she sniffed resolutely. 'Are you sure you can only stay for a week, though, Wendy? This place——' she looked around '—well, I've got the feeling it's going to defeat me.'

'I like it!' Ben pronounced.

Wendy looked around thoughtfully. 'Perhaps I can squeeze in another week. Well, Miss Sutherland, the housekeeper who gave Amy such a fright appears to have gone walkabout.'

'Do call me Sarah,' Sarah murmured. 'Mrs Tibbs will have gone to collect the milk; she always does at this time. Would you like to come and see the schoolhouse?'

'I don't want to *start* school today!' Ben declared.

'Oh, there's no chance of that,' Sarah replied. 'It's Saturday.'

Several hours later Sarah sat on the front steps of her very basic wooden cottage that adjoined the school-house and watched the Land Rover, with Wendy Wilson at the wheel, drive away. She'd not only given Wendy, Amy and co. a tour of the schoolhouse but had borrowed one of the property vehicles so that she could introduce them to the wives and show them the mustering yards, the horse paddocks, the machinery shed and so on. Whether it had been a success, whether she had accomplished what Cliff Wyatt had expected her to was debatable.

There were ten men employed permanently on Edgeleigh, four of them with wives who between them provided her twelve regular pupils, and there was Mrs Tibbs, an institution on the property. She *was* a huge, formidable woman who could rope a calf single-handedly yet had the lightest hand for making pastry and, although no one called her anything but Mrs Tibbs, the whereabouts of Mr Tibbs remained a mystery. They'd finally run her to ground at the cottage of Jean Lawson, wife of the station foreman, and Sarah had attempted to establish some sort of bridge between the newcomers and the two old hands, but although Jean Lawson had tried her hardest Mrs Tibbs had remained inscrutable and unforthcoming—although she had, Sarah had noticed, allowed her gaze to rest on the children, particularly Sally, several times. Mrs Tibbs had a very soft spot for children.

Well, I can't do any more, Sarah thought, and shook her head ruefully. As a matter of fact he's jolly lucky I did as much after what he said to me, let alone Ms Wendy Wilson's patronising ways...

And she fell to thinking about her new employer. He would be in his middle thirties, she judged, and immediately thought bitterly, Why didn't I make some comment about him not being married, which he obviously isn't? In fact I've been *told* he isn't by everyone who got into such a flutter when he bought the place!

She grimaced then propped her chin on her hands and let her mind roam backwards. As soon as it was known that Edgeleigh had changed hands much speculation had taken place. Once it had become known that the wealthy Wyatt family had bought it, the speculation had become tinged with reverence. Sarah herself had had no knowledge of them but then she was not even a Queenslander, let alone an expert on the great pastoral families of the state. But she'd swiftly become apprised of the fact that they owned other stations—Coorilla had been mentioned often in the context of being a showplace and the Wyatts' home base—and it had been said that if anyone could turn Edgeleigh's fortunes around Cliff Wyatt was the one.

'I wouldn't be surprised,' she murmured drily to herself, 'but that doesn't mean to say he's anything

but a *thoroughly* unpleasant macho type of man.'
Then she sighed and looked around. Edgeleigh had
been her home for the past year; situated in western
Queensland, it spanned thousands of acres and ran
thousands of head of cattle. It was intensely hot in
summer and could be brisk and chilly in winter, with
cold nights. It was not the most beautiful place on
earth unless you appreciated the often dry and arid
countryside and to do that you needed a fairly subtle
eye for colour. The greens weren't lush and brilliant
and sandy brown predominated but there were shades
of it that were sometimes closer to ochre, sometimes
blindingly pale, and shades of blue to the sky that
could be breathtaking. There was always an unlimited
feeling of space. And in spring there was the unbelievable glory of the wild flowers that bloomed and
cloaked the earth in blues and yellows, purples and
pinks...

But it wasn't only the colours and space Sarah had
become addicted to, it was the freedom of having her
own school, she had to acknowledge, and she caught
her breath suddenly, knowing it would be an awful
wrench to leave.

At twenty-six, she had no steady relationship with
a man, it was true, but she rarely felt it as a lack in
her life. For one thing she had reason to be somewhat
cynical about what went on between men and women;
for another she was passionate about teaching and
knowledge—for yet another she was heavily into creative arts such as papier mâché, rug-making, *de-
coupage* et cetera, she was a fine seamstress, a creative
cook, she loved growing things and grew her own
herbs and anything else she could get to grow in pots,
and she was the one who always got landed with any

sick or stray wildlife such as orphaned baby kanga-roos or koalas, and birds with broken wings.

Consequently her cottage was a riot of colour from her artistic and potted gardening endeavours—indeed they spilled over into the schoolhouse next door—and more often than not there was an inquisitive lame joey about the place, and she rarely had a free moment.

Yes, very hard to leave, she mused with a sigh, and thought of "her" school. Although the permanent number of pupils was twelve currently, she had a wandering population that sometimes doubled the ranks, of children and even occasionally adults from the mostly aboriginal pool of stockmen and ringers who came and went like the seasons. She never turned anyone away even when she knew they'd be here today gone tomorrow, and it was amazing how many of those children turned up again and again. But for her twelve permanents, she was more than just the teacher; she was the confidante of their parents, often the babysitter, sometimes the relief nurse, the adviser who knew a bit about the big cities some of them had never seen, and lots more.

At present she was even the dressmaker, she thought with a wry little smile as she got up and wandered inside towards an improvised dressmaker's dummy, drew the protective sheet aside and contemplated the wedding-dress she was making for Cindy Lawson, just eighteen, about to be married to a stockman from a neighbouring station and determined to be married in a dress that would be remembered for years on Edgeleigh. It had everything, this dress, or would have when finished, Sarah thought ruefully. The basic white taffeta was in the process of being embellished with lace, with sequins and pearl beads, with ruffles and frills and bows, and it had underskirts of billowing net. And if I don't take a stand soon, poor Cindy will be so buried by it all, we won't even see her, she reflected. But at least it is all nicely sewn, she thought as she fingered a sleeve absently, and found her mind for some reason of its own returning to Cliff Wyatt— and the uncomfortable feeling she had that he'd all too readily realised his first effect on her. And that a couple of his subsequent obscure remarks had been subtle allusions to it.

Which makes him no more likeable, she thought, then glanced at her watch and decided to spend the next hour until four o'clock making sure the schoolhouse was in tip-top condition.

It was a waste of time. By four-thirty he hadn't appeared, by five-thirty she decided he wasn't going to appear although she hadn't hung around the school house all that time, but at six she closed her front door firmly against the rising chill of an autumn dusk. She prepared a chicken casserole using herbs, bacon and mushrooms, indulged herself in a rare treat—a glass of wine to soothe her feeling of being ill-used by an arrogant man—put a compact disc of Bach on to the player to help the wine along, pulled the rubber band out of her hair and ran her fingers through it, and started to sew the last, the *very* last, she told herself firmly, of the pearl beads on to Cindy Lawson's wedding-dress while her casserole cooked.

So engrossed did she become in the delicate work that when a knock sounded on her door she called absently to come in, thinking it must be one of her pupils or their parents. So she got the surprise of her life when a light, lazy voice she remembered all too

well said with reverence, 'Hallelujah! Is it possible
I've done you a grave injustice, Miss Sutherland?'

She swung round from the dressmaker's dummy
convulsively to see Cliff Wyatt standing just inside
the front door, his dark gaze riveted upon the
wedding-dress. 'What a—concoction!' he added
wryly, and drew his gaze from it to her, standing in
her socks. 'But you know,' he mused as he took in
her loose hair and the lovely pink and gold quilted
sleeveless jacket she'd put on for warmth, 'I could
picture you in something . . . simpler?'

Sarah closed her mouth with a click, bit the cotton
thread and put her needle carefully into a pin-cushion
before she said arctically, 'It's not mine, Mr Wyatt,
so neither did you do me an injustice nor are any as-
persions you care to cast at my taste in fashion going
to do anything other than bounce harmlessly off me.'

'My apologies,' he said gravely. 'So you make
wedding-dresses in your spare time?'

'No, I don't,' she said crossly. 'Well, I am doing
this one in my spare time but it's the first. It's Cindy
Lawson's. You may have noticed that this part of the
world is not densely populated by dressmakers so
I . . . well, offered to help out.'

He laughed. 'As a matter of fact I've had that fact
rammed down my throat with monotonous, mad-
dening consistency today—I mean the lack of dressmakers, hairdressers, beauticians, manicurists,
boutiques—and the like. My sister does not believe
she can live without them these days,' he added with
less than humour.

'Well, I should have thought that would have been
obvious to you *before* today,' Sarah said candidly.

'True,' he agreed drily. 'What was not so obvious was that she would take it into her head at this highly inconvenient time to decide she was a much maligned wife and to come running home to me.'

Sarah shrugged as if it was none of her business, which it wasn't, and said curtly, 'If you've come to check out the schoolhouse, it's all locked up and you're about three hours late.'

'It seems I need to apologise again,' he replied pleasantly, 'which I do. I got caught up in other things and away from a phone.'

'Oh.' Sarah gazed at him and discovered what it felt like to have the wind taken out of your sails. 'Well...' she paused, then reached for her boots '...I suppose I could unlock it—uh—my casserole! If you wouldn't mind waiting while I take it out of the oven——'

'No, don't do that—is that what's creating such a delicious aroma?—and don't bother to struggle into your boots again,' he said politely. 'I really only came to explain that I'd been held up; we can do our tour another time. But there is something you could do for me,' he said, his gaze wandering around the colourful room and coming to rest on the open wine bottle on the counter that divided the living-area from the kitchen. 'You could offer me a drink.'

Sarah blinked then took her glasses off and rubbed her eyes. 'You . . . want to sit down and have a drink with me?' she said cautiously as she put her glasses back on.

'Why not?' he queried. 'It sounds like an essentially civilised thing to do. I also like Bach.'

'Very well,' Sarah said with a little tilt of her chin, because although there was no outward manifestation of it she knew perfectly well that he was laughing at her and would succeed in making her feel churlish and petty if she expressed any further reluctance—damn him! she thought darkly. 'I was having a glass of wine; it's nothing outstanding but it's all there is——'

'So you better just drink it and behave yourself, Mr Wyatt,' he said softly. 'I'll do my best, ma'am.' And he had the gall to sit himself down in an armchair and offer her a bland, innocent expression.

She went to get another glass with all the composure she could muster, and took her casserole out anyway because it was ready. But finally there was nothing left to do but sit down opposite him after handing him his glass, and rack her brains for something to say.

He said it for her. 'Were you born to this kind of life, Miss Sutherland?'

Surprise caused her to lift an eyebrow. 'No. Why do you ask?'

'You seem to be extremely competent at it.'

'I like it,' Sarah said slowly. 'For one thing,' she went on with a little spark of irony in her blue eyes, 'as you so rightly surmised, I'm...well, I love teaching——'

'You could teach just as well in a city.'

'But I couldn't have my own school.'

'I see,' he said thoughtfully. 'But there must be other things you like about the place?'

'Oh, there are. They're just a bit hard to put into words,' she said non-committally and sipped her wine.

His lips twisted. 'I wouldn't have thought that was often a problem for you.' And he waited.

Sarah frowned then said with some asperity, 'Why do I get the feeling this is lapsing into the kind of discussion we had this morning?'

'It could be,' he drawled, 'that, while I'm trying to draw you out in a very friendly sort of manner, you are resisting strongly. Very strongly for the rather small person you are, in fact. But of course I should have realised that smallness in stature and smallness of spirit are two very different things; indeed, I should have realised it from the moment you offered to punch me in the mouth.'

Sarah stared at him steadily for a long moment but no blinding revelations came her way. He looked only minimally less vital than he had in the morning—as if he was enjoying the opportunity to relax—and he looked absolutely no less wildly attractive for being able to rest his broad shoulders lazily back in her arm chair, stretch his long legs out and return her steady regard with just the suspicion of a wickedly amused little glint in his dark eyes. She said at last, 'Perhaps I don't forgive and forget that easily.'

'Ah. Well, may I say that you look much less like a born and bred school-marm than you did this morning?' His gaze rested on her loose hair that had a tendency to be full and wayward when unconfined and show off the golden glints in its brownness more, as well as highlight her delicate bone-structure, then his gaze drifted to her hands, which were slim and elegant, and her narrow, also elegant feet in plain white socks—which she immediately tried to tuck out of sight. 'Yes,' he mused, 'not so prim and proper or fighting mad. Have you ever thought of wearing contact lenses? Your eyes are a rather lovely blue.'

A tinge of colour stole into Sarah's cheeks but she forced herself to say coolly, 'Flattery will get you nowhere, Mr Wyatt. I adjusted to not being a raving beauty years ago.'

'There's that old saying about beauty being in the eye of the beholder,' he murmured thoughtfully. 'It seems rather—inexplicable to me that your domesticity alone hasn't made some man want to take you for his wife.'

The colour in her cheeks increased. 'If that's trying to draw me out in a very friendly manner,' she said curtly, 'I'd hate to think how you'd do it when you're feeling hostile.'

He shrugged and looked at her with a faint, genuine frown. 'I don't know why but you strike me as something of an enigma, Miss Sutherland.'

'No, I'm not, I'm perfectly normal!' she was goaded into saying. 'However I may look to you, for example,' she went on scathingly, 'I would rather die than be married for my domesticity.'

'So you believe in love, grand passions—and all that kind of thing?'

'*Yes*...' Sarah stopped and bit her lip.

'Has it ever happened for you?'

'No...look, why are we talking about it?' she said with a mixture of confusion and irritation. 'It's got nothing whatsoever to do with you!'

'All the same, it relieves my mind,' he said sweetly, and drained his glass. 'I don't suppose...' he paused and glanced at her assessingly ' ... it would cross *your* mind to offer me some of that tantalising casserole?'

'It would *not*. Why don't you go home? I'm sure Mrs Tibbs has something just as tantalising.'

'Ah, home and Mrs Tibbs,' he mused. 'Amy was in tears the last time I looked in, so was Sally in sympathy—a habit of little girls, one wonders? Be that as it may, Wendy and Mrs Tibbs were circling each other like wary tigresses and Ben had allowed the bathtub to overflow. Not an essentially peaceful place, home, at the moment.'

'My heart bleeds for you.'

He laughed and his dark eyes were so amused that it did something quite strange to Sarah, she discovered; it made her feel oddly breathless for one thing. He also said, 'You're certainly a worthy opponent, Miss Sutherland—OK, I'll consider myself banished. Goodnight.' And he got up with all the easy grace he was capable of. 'Uh—I thought of having a barbecue tomorrow night, for everyone on the property. Care to come?'

'I . . . thank you very much,' Sarah said stiffly.

'Good girl,' he responded lightly. 'You wouldn't do me another favour, would you?'

Sarah rose too and looked at him warily.

He smiled faintly. The room wasn't large and they were standing quite close together so she had to look up at him from her height of five feet three, and was unaccountably struck by the memory of him saying that, if he couldn't pick her up with one hand, he certainly could with two, and by the little tremor that the thought of it sent through her body.

'*What*?' she said tersely as all this occurred to her.

'Oh, nothing desperate or dangerous,' he said gravely, his eyes taking in the wary, troubled expression in hers. 'Not even anything mildly or wildly immoral.'

She could have shot herself as she blushed vividly this time.

'No,' he went on. 'I just wondered if you would be so good as to . . . liaise, I guess is the right word, between Amy and Mrs Tibbs and whoever else needs to be liaised with to make this barbecue a success. I would like to think it might be instrumental in helping us all to get to know each other better and, consequently, working together better.'

'All right,' Sarah said.

'Thanks. Goodnight, Miss Sutherland,' he said formally, but what lurked in his eyes was that wicked amusement again and, to her horror, Sarah discovered she had absolutely no answer for it other than to turn away with a muttered goodnight herself.

It was while she was eating her dinner that she discovered to her further horror that she felt unsettled and lonely. But why you should be feeling like this after encountering a man who is quite shamelessly taking advantage of the effect he probably has on every woman he comes in contact with is a mystery! she thought angrily. And he is doing that. Why else would he say the things he has, express any kind of interest in me? No, it's got to be . . . a game. And even if I did sort of fuel it this morning, I had cause!

'So,' she murmured militantly, 'don't think you're going to get the better of me, Mr Cliff Wyatt!'

CHAPTER TWO

'THIS is very kind of you, Sarah,' Wendy Wilson said.

'Not at all,' Sarah replied as she sat at the home-stead kitchen table drinking some of Mrs Tibbs' excellent coffee the next morning. 'Mr Wyatt asked me to help out if I could.'

'Did he indeed?' For some reason Wendy's green eyes rested on Sarah with, if she wasn't imagining it, Sarah thought, a tinge of hostility in them.

Although it was ten o'clock, Amy appeared not to have risen yet and it was Mrs Tibbs who had given the children breakfast and made them some play dough to occupy themselves with. 'Amy,' Wendy went on to say, 'was so upset last night, we decided to let her sleep in this morning. I gather you've been apprised of her break-up with her husband?'

'Yes. I'm very sorry,' Sarah said quietly.

'And I don't suppose she'll want to be too bothered with this barbecue so I'll be deputising for her. If you could tell me what needs to be done Sarah, I'll get working.'

'All right.' Sarah hid any surprise she might have felt; there was actually little because it hadn't been hard to see from the barest acquaintance that Wendy was a much more determined and capable person than her best friend. She also looked far less exotic this morning in a pair of well-cut brown corduroy trousers, polished brown moccasins and a lightweight green jumper. Her lovely dark hair was also tied back and

25

her nails, Sarah particularly noticed, had been filed to neat, shorter ovals and the fire-engine-red polish replaced by a colourless one. 'If we give Jim Lawson a buzz, he can organise a couple of men to dig the barbecue pits, get the coals going and set up the spits. I——'

But Wendy immediately walked over to the phone on the wall, consulted the list of numbers stuck beside it and proceeded to call up the Lawsons.

Sarah couldn't help raising an eyebrow, secretly, she hoped, but discovered Mrs Tibbs looking her way with a similar expression of 'you don't say!' in her eyes. She then turned back to her sink.

It took ten minutes for Wendy and Jim Lawson to make the arrangements for the pits. Wendy particularly wanted to know where they would be dug, and why they would be dug in such a spot. Jim had obviously suggested the usual place—the square in front of the machinery shed which had some grass, a couple of huge old peppercorn trees and some permanent tables and benches, and which was the general gathering place, even the hub or the heart of the property—whereas Wendy had thought the homestead back garden more appropriate. But she finally conceded and it was arranged that they should be able to start eating at five o'clock. She came back to the kitchen table and said, 'Well, I gather the practice is to spit-roast the meat—Mrs Tibbs, would you be so kind as to select the meat from the cold room? Two men will be up to collect it. That leaves the salads, I guess,' she added.

Mrs Tibbs snorted. 'Salads! We're not feeding a party of namby-pamby fancy people on this station, miss. Salads, my word!' And she crossed her arms that were like sides of meat themselves in a gesture of outrage.

'My mistake,' Wendy murmured. 'What *do* we eat on this here station?'

Sarah intervened hastily as Mrs Tibbs opened her mouth. 'Rice is very popular. We generally have a few pots of curry or goulash, Jean Lawson makes a particularly fine potato casserole and Mrs Tibbs does a tasty dish of ground maize meal that she serves with gravy.'

'Very well,' Wendy said with just the faintest expression of distaste at the mention of maize meal. 'Perhaps you wouldn't mind ringing the Lawsons back, Sarah, and asking Jean to do her potatoes? Is it anyone's special prerogative to make the curry or goulash?'

'I make the goulash or the curry, whichever I decide on,' Mrs Tibbs pronounced, arms still akimbo.

'Then I've had a wonderful idea,' Wendy said ingeniously. 'I make a really mean curry, Mrs Tibbs, so why don't you do the goulash?'

'You mean you want to make curry here in my kitchen?'

'Yes, but I tell you what—if you don't think it's up to your curry, Mrs Tibbs, I'll feed it to the pigs or whatever you've got here as an equivalent.'

'Is that like a bet, miss?' Mrs Tibbs enquired expressionlessly.

'Yes.'

'You're on!'

'Good. Now rice——'

'I'll do the rice,' Sarah said as she struggled not to laugh.

'Excellent.' Wendy looked thoughtful for a moment. 'What does everyone drink?'

'Beer,' both Sarah and Mrs Tibbs replied, although Mrs Tibbs added,

'And you don't want to go suggesting spirits or gut-rotting wine, miss. Many a fight has started that way!'

Wendy grimaced but said nothing further on the subject. 'How many people will there be, do you think?'

'Uh ... ten, twenty-three, twenty-seven—about thirty-two; there are a couple of ringers in the camp but fourteen of those will be kids,' Sarah said.

'What a thought,' Wendy murmured.

'It's all right. I usually take care of the kids. We play games and so on until the food is ready. If we're eating at five we generally collect an hour or so earlier——' Sarah stopped as Amy trailed into the kitchen in a beautiful silk housecoat but sporting a pale, woebegone expression.

'I suppose it's too much to hope this barbecue is off?' she said petulantly.

At four o'clock that afternoon Sarah was at the bar-becue area, as were most of the other employees, but there was no sign of the homestead party as yet. And she detected a certain amount of tension that was not normally present as smoke drifted through the air and the roasting carcasses were turned slowly on their spits.

It was a beautiful afternoon as the sun started to sink, with a few streaks of cloud in a sky tinged with apricot, and most of the men, cattlemen born and bred, discarded their tall hats which normally appeared glued to their heads. Most of them also wore boots with heels and silver-studded belts and, looking around, you couldn't doubt this was cowboy country, Queensland style, because, although Edgeleigh now possessed a helicopter with the word 'WYATT' painted on its side, a lot of the men had been born and bred to a saddle as well and the night paddocks with their complement of horses were not far away.

For a couple of minutes Sarah stopped what she was doing—arranging dishes on one of the wooden tables—and looked around a little dreamily. It was romantic to be stuck out so far away from anywhere, with these people with their slower but not necessarily less wise speech, their far-seeing eyes, their simple ways.

Then she noticed two Land Rovers approaching from the homestead, and everyone sat up.

It was Cliff Wyatt who contrived to break the ice in a masterly exhibition that Sarah could only applaud secretly and wonder how he'd done it. But the fact remained that in ten minutes or so he had everyone drinking and talking, he had Amy placed between Jean and Cindy Lawson and he himself with a beer in hand, and was surrounded by the men.

'Not bad,' Mrs Tibbs remarked, plonking a pot down next to Sarah's rice. 'Him I could get along with. Her—that's another matter,' she added darkly.

'Amy?'

'No! She won't stay long—the other one, with the green eyes like a cat.'

'Well, she's definitely not staying long,' Sarah offered, and had Mrs Tibbs look at her with severe contempt. 'What's that supposed to mean?' she queried with a smile curving her lips. 'Wasn't her curry any good?'

'Her curry is bloody good,' Mrs Tibbs said. 'That doesn't mean I have to like her.'

'I still don't see how it's going to be a problem,' Sarah said with a faint frown.

'Then I'll spell it out for you even though you're the teacher round here—she plans to be Mrs Cliff Wyatt one day, you mark my words.'

Sarah's lips parted and her eyes widened. 'Oh...' she said very slowly.

'Yep, makes sense, doesn't it? Well, maybe not to the likes of you, right off, leastwise, being a bit naïve on these subjects——'

'I am not!' Sarah protested.

'Course you are,' Mrs Tibbs replied indulgently. 'Hasn't the veterinarian been making eyes at you for months—but have you noticed? Seems to me not.'

Sarah swallowed in an unusually flustered way as she thought of Tim Markwell, whom she liked, but not in that way. 'He hasn't!'

'Who hasn't?' Wendy Wilson asked as she delivered another pot to the table from the Land Rover. 'My curry,' she added gently. 'Mrs Tibbs has allowed me to present it. Sarah, you can do either of two things for me—help Amy out a bit or help Sally and Ben out by starting to organise the kids.'

Sarah controlled an urge to tell Wendy Wilson to go to hell and said stiffly, 'Right, I'll do the kids.'

Whereas Mrs Tibbs said to the world at large, 'What did I tell you?'

It was a successful barbecue. Almost from the first Ben joined in the games with vigour and initiative and even Sally released Sarah's hand eventually and consented to be part of things. And when the meal was served Sarah had them all sitting in a ring so that they ate in a fairly orderly manner but with much enjoyment and it was only when they'd all finished that she released them to run wild a bit in the firelit darkness to play an energetic game of Cowboys and Indians. And Wendy contrived to hold court with the wives and older daughters in an exhibition almost as masterly as Cliff Wyatt's that all the same irritated Sarah for reasons that weren't that easy to identify. At least, she did acknowledge honestly to herself, the other girl rubbed her up the wrong way, so whatever she did would probably be irritating, however well she did it.

But surely why this was so could have nothing to do with Wendy's ambition to be Mrs Cliff Wyatt— or could it? she asked herself once then shook her head in a gesture of disbelief, but added to herself, I don't even know if it's true and not an odd fancy of Mrs Tibbs'! But the irony of that thought made her feel curiously uncomfortable so she resolutely closed her mind to the whole subject.

It was a lot harder to keep her mind closed when she was presented with undeniable verification of Mrs Tibbs' theory that same evening.

She'd helped Mrs Tibbs clear up after the barbecue—Amy had taken herself and the children to bed and Wendy and Cliff had disappeared. And after they'd scoured the last pot they had a cup of tea in the big kitchen, then Sarah yawned, said goodnight and let herself out of the back door to make her way home. It was about a quarter of a mile to her cottage and she pulled her jacket around her and rubbed her hands as she descended the back steps and walked around the house. The night was clear, starry and cold and she walked soundlessly on the grass for a few yards until she heard voices and stopped uncertainly. They were coming from above and in front of her, from the veranda, and she immediately recognised Wendy's voice—not only her voice but what she was saying and the way she was saying it...

'You must admit I did well tonight, darling.'

'Very well,' Cliff Wyatt answered.

'Surely I deserve a bit more than that for...slaying so many dragons in a manner of speaking?' Every husky, sexy intonation of Wendy's voice carried clearly on the cold night air.

'What did you have in mind?'

'This,' she said, and Sarah couldn't help herself. Her eyes had adjusted to the darkness and she could see both Wendy and Cliff Wyatt—not in any great detail but their outlines—and she saw Wendy move into his arms and gaze up into his eyes. They stood like that for a long moment then she saw Cliff Wyatt's dark head lower to the paler glimmer of Wendy's up-turned face and their lips meet.

That was when she turned and slipped away around the other side of the house.

'But do *you* believe in Father Christmas, Miss Sutherland?' Billy Pascoe said. He was a thin, intense, trouble-prone child with awkward dark hair that seemed to grow straight upwards and resisted his mother's every attempt to tame it.

'Well, it's generally only little people who believe in Father Christmas, the tooth fairy and the Easter Bunny, Billy, but I must admit that last Christmas I could have sworn I saw someone who looked *exactly* like Father Christmas getting around Edgeleigh on a horse——'

'You always tell us we're not allowed to swear, miss!'

'Yes, I do but this is a different kind of swearing and has nothing to do with the saying of rude words——'

'Anyway, he's supposed to be on a reindeer and that was——'

'Perhaps his reindeer were sick, Billy,' Sarah interposed smoothly. 'And now, as it's two minutes to three and nearly time for the bell, you can collect the art books, Billy—Billy,' she said calmly, and outstared him firmly until he subsided grudgingly and did as he was told. 'And you, Ben, can put away the paints.'

Ben sprang up and did so obligingly—anything to do with art and painting appealed to Ben—then he said, looking over Sarah's shoulder. 'Oh, here's Uncle Cliff!'

Sarah didn't turn but reached for the bell and swung it. 'All right, off you go.'

Cliff Wyatt waited until they'd all tumbled out of the schoolhouse before he said anything. Then he strolled in front of her and remarked, 'That was a masterpiece of diplomacy, Miss Sutherland. I quite thought he'd got you over the matter of swearing.'

Sarah grimaced. 'It's the likes of Billy Pascoe who keep teachers honest. How long were you there?'

He grinned. 'Not long—you seem to have a large proportion of under-nines in your school.'

'I have three teenagers actually but there's an exam coming up so I gave them study leave after lunch. It's easier for them to work at home sometimes.'

'Any budding geniuses?' he queried.

Sarah shrugged. 'I don't know about that but Donald Lawson, Cindy's brother, is very bright and should be able to go on to university—with a bit of luck.'

'Such as?'

'His father's approval,' she said quietly. 'Jim is still a bit staggered, I think, to find he has a son who is more interested in the Theory of Relativity than cattle. And, to be honest, I'm getting out of my depth a little. He should be at a proper high school with a science department but——' she smiled briefly '—I'm sure they'll work it out. Have you come for your tour of the facilities? Where would you like to start?' she added briskly.

He studied her for a moment with a faint frown in his eyes then said, 'Perhaps not.'

Sarah eyed him exasperatedly. '*Why* not?'

'I don't think this would be a good time for it.'

'It's a much better time now that school's finished rather than sneaking up on me when I've got Billy Pascoe pinning me to the wall about Father Christmas in front of a whole lot of younger kids,' she said crossly.

'So that's why you're angry? But I thought you handled it very well——'

'I'm not—angry,' Sarah denied frustratedly and none too truthfully.

'Constrained, then?' he suggested. 'As if I've done something to alienate you further?'

Sarah stared at him and discovered that her heart was beating oddly with a little pulse of panic. Surely he couldn't have divined her peculiarly ambiguous

state of mind since she'd witnessed him kissing Wendy
Wilson on the veranda last night?

'You'd be better off telling me,' he said after a
strangely tense little pause.

Sarah came to life. 'No! I mean no, there's nothing.
Look, I'm quite fine actually so why don't we get it
over and done with . . . ?' She trailed off on a lowering
note as she realised how *that* sounded. 'Oh, hell,' she
added hollowly, 'perhaps you're right.'

What he would have said then was to remain a
mystery because as he looked her over with the frown
still in his eyes Ben and Sally popped back into the
schoolhouse demanding to know if he'd come to fetch
them or what. 'Yes,' he said slowly, 'why not?' And
added expressionlessly, 'Another day, then, Miss
Sutherland?'

'Thank you. Yes. Whenever it suits you,' Sarah said
and groaned inwardly at how craven *that* sounded.

It was two weeks before she had anything more than
passing contact with Cliff Wyatt but it was impossible
to be unaware of his presence daily on the property.
Her pupils and their parents were full of his doings,
the changes he was making, and there was an air of
hope and expectancy about the place rather than the
sad feeling of whistling against the wind that had pre-
vailed before it was sold.

It also became evident that Cliff Wyatt was not all
sweetness and light, as Sarah could have told them,
but an exacting boss who expected everyone to give
their best and who could be coldly, cuttingly and sar-
donically unpleasant in a devastatingly accurate
manner when they didn't. Nevertheless, this on the

whole engendered a spirit of respect, she judged—and
discovered that that irritated her as well.

All in all, she thought with a sigh once, the wretched
man has contrived to set me on an uneven keel and
I can't seem to right myself. If I didn't have to hear
so much about him it might help and, of course, if I
didn't have to see him at all, that would help even
more...

But it was not so easy to avoid seeing Cliff Wyatt
although it was generally at a distance, but, even so,
his height and easy carriage made him unmistakable,
as did his air of authority, and, whether he was riding
a horse, climbing into the helicopter which he piloted
himself sometimes or simply striding to and from the
homestead, she not only saw him often but felt the
same stupid impact as she had the first time she'd laid
eyes on him.

Of course it has to go away, she told herself more
than once. I'm twenty-six! I'm not a giddy girl—and
I don't like him. You simply can't be a rational adult
and be obsessed with a man you don't like...

That was how, unfortunately, as it turned out, on
one of the occasions when she did come into contact
with him briefly she also came to be more friendly
than usual towards Tim Markwell, the vet, who was
with him when they all met as she was shepherding
the children back from a ramble they'd taken as part
of a nature-study class.

Tim was not as tall as Cliff Wyatt but good-looking
in a quiet way with a kind, gentle manner towards
animals and humans alike. He flew his own plane
from Longreach where he was based and his surgery
covered hundreds of square miles. He was in his early
thirties, she judged, and it was only after she'd bes-

towed a particularly warm smile upon him that she found herself hoping against hope that Mrs Tibbs had been *wrong*, and remembering uneasily that she'd been right about Wendy Wilson, though.

'Hi, Sarah,' Tim said easily but with a faint tinge of surprise in his eyes. 'Been studying the local flora and fauna?'

'Yes,' she said wryly, 'and I'm all talked out on the subject.' In fact she did feel a bit tired, she realised, but for no real reason that she could fathom.

'Why don't you give them an early day?' Cliff Wyatt suggested after subjecting her to a penetrating scrutiny.

'Oh, no.' Sarah looked shocked. 'I couldn't do that!'

'Ah, but I could,' he said, and turned to address the group of kids, who, delighted at their stroke of good fortune, needed no further invitation to scamper off delightedly.

'How could you do that?' Sarah said incredulously.

'It was quite simple,' he replied gravely but with a tinge of irony.

'Well, you shouldn't have!'

'Why not? A couple of hours off isn't going to harm them and it might even do you a bit of good.'

'But it's undermining my authority!'

'I doubt it,' he drawled. 'Don't you think you're over-reacting?' he added politely but in a way that somehow caused her to squirm inwardly and feel shrewish, and also added force to his point that she needed a break.

'Perhaps you're right,' she said abruptly and turned away.

'Oh, by the way, Sarah,' Tim said. 'That sick wombat that I took to the surgery has recovered completely and is in a fair way to becoming the bane of my life! He eats shoes and socks.'

Sarah turned back with a smile lighting her face. 'Oh, I'm so pleased, Tim! Not about the shoes and socks but that he's recovered. What will you do with him?'

'I've got the feeling I'm stuck with him,' Tim said ruefully. 'Unless you'd like him back?'

Sarah grimaced. 'I'm not sure that I could cope with a naughty wombat on top of—well, some naughty kids.'

'Then I'll spare you that fate!'

She spent that afternoon working on Cindy's dress and taking herself to task over the image she appeared to be projecting of a slightly rattled teacher.

Three days later she was summoned to the homestead and arrived to find Amy in tears, Wendy still in residence and Cliff Wyatt in an unpleasant, cutting mood.

'Sit down, Sarah.' They were assembled in the main lounge-cum-dining-room, a large, graceful room with a high ceiling and a wooden archway dividing it. The furniture, she noted in a quick glance around, was beautiful; there was a round mahogany dining-table with a central pedastal and eight chairs, a studded leather lounge suite and two exquisite Persian carpets on the restored wooden floor.

'We've asked you to come up and give us your opinion as to whether Sally and Ben can be left here for a couple of weeks without their mother,' Cliff Wyatt said.

Sarah blinked and Amy said tearfully, 'Do you have to make it sound so awful? As if I really am abandoning them?'

'I'm not doing anything of the kind,' he replied in clipped tones. 'What would be quite ridiculous, to my mind, is the idea of you carting them off for an indefinite period, upsetting their schooling and generally unsettling them all round while you try to get your life back together. Sarah——' he turned to her '—as if it isn't obvious, how are they settling in?'

Sarah said slowly, 'Very well. Ben can be a bit of a handful at times but that's nothing unusual for little boys, especially bright little boys. And now I've discovered he has quite a flair for art and loves to paint I've been giving him some extra art lessons, which he loves. As for Sally, she's made a friend, they're inseparable actually, and got over a lot of her shyness. I'd say they're both happy and well-adjusted at the moment.'

'And we can't lay much of the responsibility for that at your door these days, Amy,' her brother said pointedly.

The result was inevitable. Amy started to sob convulsively and Wendy murmured, 'Cliff, I don't think this is helping much.'

Sarah stood up. 'I'll——'

'Sit down,' Cliff Wyatt ordered.

But Sarah stood her ground with a little glint of anger in her eyes. 'This has nothing to do with me,' she replied evenly, and in truth, although she couldn't help feeling some impatience with the ever-tearful Amy, she also couldn't help feeling a bit sorry for her.

'It has in the sense that if Amy could be assured of your interest in Sally and Ben she might go with a clearer conscience.'

Sarah returned his hard, probing look with a rather old-fashioned one of her own. 'Naturally I'm interested in them,' she said stiffly, 'and if Mrs Tibbs needs a hand at all I'd be happy to help——'

'Good, that's settled, then,' Cliff Wyatt said decisively but Amy only sobbed harder and Sarah glared at him then walked over to the other girl and said gently,

'They'll be fine with us for a while, Amy. But I think you should let them know that it won't be for long, and you should make every effort to be calm and loving before you go.'

'I'll try—I will!' Amy wailed. 'Oh, thank you, Sarah! I know Mrs Tibbs is very good with them but you're such a sensible sort of person. I've watched you with the kids and so on...' And she resolutely blew her nose, swallowed several times and managed a shaky smile.

'The very personification of it,' Cliff Wyatt murmured, while Sarah thought two thoughts—that she'd been unaware of Amy's approval or that she'd even been interested enough to notice anything, and, secondly, to wonder what she was getting herself into.

CHAPTER THREE

AMY and Wendy departed a day and a half later and for the next couple of days Sarah watched Ben and Sally with extra care but could detect no trauma. And on the third day after their mother's departure they arrived at school, bustling with importance and an invitation for Sarah to have dinner that night at the homestead.

She groaned inwardly but, looking at their eager faces, knew she couldn't refuse although she would have dearly loved to because she was still filled with indignation directed squarely towards Cliff Wyatt for his high-handed ways.

But the early dinner they shared with the children was a pleasant meal, and something became obvious that hadn't occurred to her before—Sally and Ben were clearly very fond of their uncle. And she helped Mrs Tibbs put them to bed, read them a story then went to find her host to bid him goodnight, only to find that Mrs Tibbs had made coffee for them and served it in the lounge.

'I——'

'Sit down, Sarah,' Cliff Wyatt said with a tinge of humour. 'There's no need to dash off; I'm really not the ogre you take me for.'

She hesitated but as he poured her coffee she sat and accepted it with a quiet word of thanks.

'So. No problems with our temporary orphans, I gather?'

'None that I can see,' she replied. 'Has . . . have you heard from Amy?'

'Yes. She rings every day. She's staying with Wendy but I'm not sure that's such a good thing.'

Sarah raised an eyebrow at him.

'Wendy is a very . . . assured person,' he said thoughtfully. 'Amy never has been and for her to try to practise Wendy's philosophies regarding love, men and marriage . . .' He shrugged.

'They seem to be such good friends, though.'

'They've known each other since primary school but, whereas Amy got herself into marriage and motherhood when she might have been too young to know what she was doing, Wendy has been a career girl. To date,' he added.

Sarah frowned faintly as she tried to analyse his tone but it proved impossible so she sat in silence for a while then heard herself say, a little to her surprise, 'What's Amy's husband like?'

It took about a minute for Cliff Wyatt to reply. Then he said drily, 'The strange thing is, he's a good friend of mine and works for me.'

'Oh.'

'Yes,' Cliff agreed wryly. 'Rather awkward. And, while he may not be the finest husband in the world, he's not an ogre either. But something has gone out of it for them obviously and she is my sister.'

'I'm glad to hear you say that,' Sarah murmured.

He glinted an amused look across at her. 'What prompted that? Your membership of the universal club of women? Or the conviction that blood should be thicker than water?'

'Both probably,' Sarah said caustically.

'So if I were to tell you that my real conviction on the subject of Amy and Ross is that it's about time she settled down and stopped looking for moonlight and roses around every corner, stopped worrying more about hairdressers and clothes than being a mother and a wife she would be a lot better off—if I were to tell you all that, no doubt you'd take instant umbrage?'

Sarah looked across at him coolly. 'Not at all. But I would make the comment that it's probably impossible to know exactly what goes on between a man and a woman and only a fool would imagine he does.'

'Ah, well, I'd be surprised if I was wrong but,' he drawled, apparently in no way put out, 'that's quite a list you're compiling, Sarah.'

She frowned. 'I don't know what you mean.'

'You've called me a fool, an underminer of your authority—oh, and let's not forget what an aggressively, unpleasantly macho type I am. But tell me something—what goes on between you and Tim Markwell?'

The unexpectedness of it caused Sarah some confusion and caused some colour to come to her cheeks. 'That's none of your business...*nothing*!' she said disjointedly.

'Then there's no need to protest so much,' he said lazily. 'But I thought you'd be quite well-suited.'

Sheer anger all but took Sarah's breath away. 'You know nothing about it,' she shot at him. 'You're just being...'

He lifted a wry eyebrow and waited a moment. 'Another damning epithet? I don't mind, you know. In fact I enjoy our little sparring matches.'

Sarah ground her teeth but before she could say anything he went on leisurely, 'I'm just not quite sure why I have this—ability to enrage you so much whereas Tim apparently doesn't. Hence my question.'

'Every second thing you say is calculated to enrage me one way or another,' Sarah replied coldly.

He laughed softly. 'So it would seem. But in point of fact, for example, I'd be much happier to see Amy spending some time here with you and getting down to a few of the basics of life—now that surely has to be a compliment?'

Sarah stood up. 'Depends which way you look at it,' she said. 'If you're implying, *for example*, that I'm such a down-to-earth, mundane sort of person for whom moonlight and roses might never exist——'

'Sarah——' he stood up as well and looked down at her gravely '—I think you should give Tim a bit more encouragement—I say that because it seems to me you're exhibiting all the classic symptoms of a girl who has gone too much the other way—the opposite way to Amy, I mean—and that you're actually dying for a bit of moonlight and roses.'

Sarah's lips parted and she was struck speechless by his sheer effrontery, speechless but stiff with outrage that was stamped into every taut line of her body. She longed to hit him.

'And that,' he murmured, his gaze suddenly narrowed and rather intent, 'is where you slap my face, I gather, Miss Sutherland. Now what would be a fitting finale to such a scenario? I could always retaliate by pulling you into my arms and kissing you breathless.'

'D-don't you dare!' she stammered.

'Why not?' he drawled. 'I'm quite as capable as Tim Markwell of providing some moonlight and roses, I should imagine—why don't we put it to the test?' And, without waiting for a reply and before she could guess his intentions, he removed her glasses so that not only was she besieged by a maelstrom of emotions but she was suddenly at the acute disadvantage of having to peer up at him short-sightedly. Nor was anything relieved when he said softly, 'That's much better, and much more comfortable for doing this, I'm sure.'

'This', as she moved convulsively and opened her mouth agitatedly, was to be drawn into his arms and have his lips seek hers.   .

'No, no!' she protested. 'You mustn't—Mr Wyatt! Please . . .'

'You're probably quite right—I shouldn't,' he said against the corner of her mouth as he moved his hands on her back. 'But the fact remains I'm going to—I don't know why but you rather intrigue me, Miss Sutherland. Is it possible that you're still a virgin?'

She gasped and tried to wrench herself free but, without exerting a lot of effort, he kept her in his arms and when she stopped struggling merely gathered her close again, quite gently, and started to kiss her.

Five minutes later, they separated and Sarah put a hand to her mouth and said helplessly, 'Oh, this is terrible!'

'No, it's not,' he contradicted but in an entirely different voice and kept his hands on her waist until she was steady on her feet. Then he let her go and she looked around blindly with her hands pressed to her cheeks.

'Here.' He handed her her glasses.

She took them wordlessly and as everything swung back into focus as she put them on unsteadily she found him looking down at her with that narrowed, thoughtful look she was coming to know and a fresh wave of colour poured into her cheeks.

She opened her mouth but he forestalled her. 'Sit down, Sarah. I'll pour you some more coffee.'

She breathed unevenly and said jerkily, 'No. I'll go——'

'You'll do as you're told.' And he simply put his hands around her waist and deposited her in the chair behind her. 'Here,' he said again, a few moments later, and put a cup of coffee down beside her. 'Drink it,' he added quietly and turned away to pour a cup for himself.

She closed her eyes and licked her lips then drank some coffee and after a few moments felt herself calming a little. By this time he was sitting opposite her with his own cup and when she allowed their gazes to meet at last she said with a strange mixture of desolation and reproach, 'You shouldn't have done that.' And could have shot herself for not being able to come up with something more positive.

'Probably not,' he replied consideringly, his dark gaze holding hers captive, 'but you have to admit it had its moments.'

She felt hot all over again and looked down at the cup in her hands but was relieved to discover that she also suddenly felt fierce and ill-used. So she said tartly, 'Well, I do hope you're not going to make too much of that, Mr Wyatt, because you'd be making a big mistake if you did.'

He smiled fleetingly. 'Would I? I don't know,' he mused. '*Are* you a virgin, Sarah?'

She tightened her lips and said precisely, 'I'll tell you what I am, Mr Wyatt——'

'I think you should call me Cliff,' he broke in with another, this time wry, little smile. 'Otherwise we could sound as if we've stepped out of *Pride and Prejudice*.'

'I'll tell you what I am, Mr Wyatt,' Sarah repeated deliberately. 'I'm in the situation of having had myself taken advantage of intolerably!'

'Intolerably?' He lifted an eyebrow at her. 'Forgive me but I quite thought you enjoyed having such—intolerable advantage taken of you.'

Sarah bit her lip. 'Well,' she said, 'well…whatever, but all the same…' and she paused to cast him a chilly glance ' …how would you describe the situation of a woman who found herself being kissed merely on a whim? Because I certainly didn't instigate it, I have no doubt it was only a whim on your part and I also happened to witness you kissing Wendy Wilson only a couple of weeks ago,' she said scornfully, 'so don't try and tell me you're anything but a . . .' She stopped, lost for the right word.

'Ah, so that explains it,' Cliff Wyatt murmured. 'A thorough, two-timing bastard, you were going to say?' he enquired politely. 'That's two new ones to add to your repertoire.'

Sarah glared at him. 'Explains *what*?'

'Why you've viewed me like some sort of un-pleasant sub-life lately—by the way I wasn't aware of your presence when I was with Wendy but, be that as it may…' He shrugged and regarded her with a wicked, quizzical little glint before continuing gently, 'I think you ought to explain whether you disapprove of my kissing her on moral grounds or personal grounds.'

Sarah swallowed suddenly as she saw the trap too late and could have died of embarrassment anyway at what she'd revealed in such a hasty, hot-headed way. Then she said tautly, 'Let's leave personalities out of this. Nor was I—snooping in any way; I just happened to be going past on my way home the night of the barbecue when, well, you and Wendy were on the veranda and I didn't realise it until too late. But talking of moral grounds, I still don't think it's unreasonable to object to being kissed when you—simply when *you*—'

'Even though you enjoyed it, Sarah?'

She took a breath and stood up. 'Goodnight, Mr Wyatt,' she said as evenly as she could.

'And here endeth the lecture,' he drawled with a mocking little glint in his eye. 'All right, go to bed, Miss Sutherland. But may I just say in my own defence that Wendy and I have no—formal contract towards each other of any kind and——?'

'And you were intrigued?' Sarah said flatly. 'I believe you.'

He laughed. 'As a matter of fact it was more a case of being kissed rather than the opposite, but I wasn't going to mention that; it didn't seem terribly gallant to do so other than in the cause of truth. Whereas I was fleetingly but quite genuinely intrigued in your case, although I'm not sure why.'

Sarah's nostrils flared. 'Of all the . . .' She stopped abruptly.

'Well, you can't have it both ways, Sarah,' he said reasonably. 'You seem to be so sure it was a thoroughly reprehensible thing to do on my part, so badly motivated, so unacceptable to you despite certain manifestations to the contrary, I can't help wondering what did intrigue me in the first place. Would you like me to walk you home?' he asked, getting up at last.

Sarah closed her mouth with a click of her teeth, swung on her heel and marched out.

She slept badly for the next few nights and suffered the consequences over the succeeding days, in the form of finding every one of her twelve charges one too many. So by five o'clock on Friday afternoon she was only too happy to be able to close herself into her house, kick off her boots and sink into an armchair.

But the real horror of it all, she decided, the awful embarrassment that made her soul cringe, was the fact that she couldn't forget those few minutes in Cliff Wyatt's arms when sheer surprise had overcome her and she'd been unable to close her mind to a kind of rapture that shouldn't, in the circumstances, have come to her. Only it had, in the form of an undeniable awareness of him, of the strength of his body but used so lightly, the . . . just the lovely feel of being in his arms, she thought despairingly, and how it made *me* feel, how it made me lose my head and kiss him back . . . How did he put it? 'It had its moments'.

She took her glasses off, laid her head back wearily and contemplated whether she *was* a bit starved of moonlight and roses. But how could it sneak up on me like this? she asked herself. I was perfectly happy until . . . *Is* it just the effect he has on women? I don't know whether that makes me feel better or worse. I don't know *why* I always get so het up when I'm with him but I suppose I do know that I'm really a sane, rather serious schoolteacher, and I'm certainly no match for Wendy Wilson in the glamour stakes—no, stop, Sarah! she commanded herself and sat up abruptly. Just . . . put it out of your mind.

The telephone rang.

She glared at the offending instrument then got up to answer it. It was Billy Pascoe's mother in a panic because Billy appeared to have disappeared.

'I'm sure he hasn't, Mary,' Sarah said soothingly but with an inward sigh because this happened on average about once a fortnight. 'I'll bet you'll find him hiding in the machinery shed.'

'I've searched every inch of the machinery shed and everywhere else!' Mary Pascoe replied distraughtly down the line. She also added accusingly, 'He said you were cross with him today over something he didn't do.'

Sarah leant against the wall tiredly and thought of the perpetual disruption Billy Pascoe was with his eternal questions and his awkward facility for being just plain awkward all the time, none of which was helped by an anxious, fussing mother and a father who drank a lot. But none of *that* altered the fact that she'd possibly been sharper with him than was warranted today and she felt a tinge of guilt. 'Where's Mike?' she asked, meaning Billy's father.

'They're camping out tonight on a muster; there's not a man around!'

'OK, Mary, I'll come over right away. I'm sure we'll find him somewhere.'

But by dawn the next morning Billy Pascoe had still not been found and, feeling guiltier and guiltier by the minute although she well knew that Billy was a genius at not being found until he wanted to be,

Sarah took a Land Rover and decided to widen the area of search. There were several abandoned sheds and structures within a two- or three-mile radius that he could, just conceivably, have walked to. She left Jean Lawson and Mrs Tibbs in charge of the mothers and children left behind and told them she'd only be away for an hour at the most.

It was to prove a thoroughly disastrous decision. The Land Rover conked out on her about as far away from the homestead as she'd planned to go and, being quite unmechanical, she had no idea what was wrong with it and decided she'd have to walk the three miles back. Then she put her foot unsuspectingly down a rabbit hole and the result was an ankle that swelled up alarmingly and started to throb painfully. She sat down on the ground, put her head in her hands and could have wept with sheer frustration.

Two hours later, when she'd hobbled a bit and sat down a lot and been burnt by the sun and was getting thirstier and thirstier, an aboriginal ringer on horseback and leading another horse found her.

'Oh, Charlie, thank heavens!' she gasped, recognising the broad face of the young aboriginal who had occasionally graced her school. 'How did you find me?'

'Followed your tracks, missus,' Charlie responded with a wide, dazzlingly white smile as he hopped off his horse and knelt down beside her. 'I ain't the best tracker round these parts for nothing,' he added with simple pride. 'Wow! You sure done hurt your ankle.'

'I know. I stepped in a rabbit hole but,' she said urgently, 'I was looking for Billy Pascoe——'

'Now don't you worry your head there, Missus Sarah,' Charlie said soothingly. 'They found him. In the roof of his own house.'

Sarah beat her fists on her knees. 'I knew it! I knew he had to have found some . . . Oh, well, that's good news, Charlie.' She grimaced with pain as he helped her up and on to the second horse. But once up and as they were walking gently side by side she was struck by another thought. 'Who . . . sent you to find me, Charlie?'

'Cliff did. I tole him I was better on a horse, he tole me, "Just bloody find her; I don't care how."' Charlie laughed cheerfully.

'He's . . . not in a good mood?' Sarah queried cautiously. 'Why did he come home?'

'See, it was like this,' Charlie said expansively. 'That crazy ringer Willy Doughboy goes and gets hisself stomped by an angry cattle early this morning and we lose the mob because they got the jitters now and decide they like to go walkabout—take another couple a days to catch 'em too!

'Anyway, the boss says to me, "You come with me, Charlie; we'll take Willie back in the chopper and call the Flying Doctor to meet us." But what happens? When we get back the Flying Doc's there all right but there's also a whole lot of women and kids running round like chooks because you gone walkabout like the cows and got yourself lost and Billy Pascoe's lost too. All make Cliff plenty mad!' he finished, and chuckled again as if the vagaries of cattle mobs, the wrath of Cliff Wyatt and everything else were but the merest pin-pricks.

Sarah looked round at the ancient landscape and for a moment was lost in admiration for the wonderful philosophy of an ancient race. But a moment later tension returned to her at the thought of facing the 'boss' in a bad mood. 'How *did* Billy get found?' she asked to distract herself.

'Think he musta heard Cliff, 'cause he just appeared suddenly. Said he'd fallen asleep and hadn't heard no one else. That kid's a right handful!'

'You're not wrong,' Sarah said feelingly as they jogged into the square in front of the machinery shed to be met by all sorts of anxious people who suddenly parted like the Red Sea as Cliff Wyatt strode towards the horses.

'Where the devil have you been, Miss Sutherland?' he said coldly, and added cuttingly, 'Wouldn't you think that one lost soul was enough without adding yourself to the list?'

Sarah was struck by several things: that her ankle was aching abominably, that Cliff Wyatt in dusty khaki and heavy boots looked as he never had to her before—like a true cattleman, and she realised this had niggled her subconsciously, but primarily she was struck by the fact that she should try to keep her temper in front of everyone. So she said carefully, 'I thought Billy might have walked to one of the abandoned sheds around the place but when I got a couple of miles away the Land Rover—uh—died on me and unfortunately I'm no mechanic; but I was *not* lost, Mr Wyatt; I would have got back eventually,' she finished coolly.

'Mighta taken you a long time,' Charlie put in, obviously quite unaware of the undercurrents. 'That there'm ankle don't look too good to me. She stepped down an ol' bunny hole,' he added.

Cliff Wyatt pulled up the leg of her jeans, swore audibly and, without so much as a by-your-leave, lifted her off the horse and started to walk away with her.

'Will you put me down, Mr Wyatt?' she commanded angrily, quite forgetting her resolve not to lose her temper.

'No, I won't—just shut up, Sarah, and do as you're told,' Cliff replied caustically, and every wildly interested child following them became pop-eyed and breathless with further excitement.

'Look *here*,' she started to say.

He stopped striding along briefly and said roughly, looking down at her with his dark eyes blazing, 'No, *you* look here, Sarah Sutherland, and just draw your claws in because I'm not carting you off to my harem as your spinsterish little soul is secretly dying for me to do anyway, I'm simply taking you to the first-aid room where the Flying Doctor is still stitching Willy Doughboy up, so he can have a look at your ankle.'

There was only one indignity left for Sarah to suffer. She quite spontaneously—she couldn't have stopped herself if she'd tried—burst into angry, frustrated tears. Whereupon Cliff Wyatt breathed deeply, raised his eyes heavenwards, swore fluently again and proceeded once more towards the first-aid room. It was at this point that everyone else decided discretion might be the better part of valour and all interested spectators melted away.

'I'm not staying here.'

Cliff folded his arms and leant his shoulders back against the door-jamb of a guest bedroom in the homestead and regarded Sarah steadily as she sat on the bed he'd just set her down upon—her sunburnt, tear-streaked face, her ragged hair and dirty clothes and finally her bound ankle. 'What do you suggest?' he enquired witheringly at last. 'You've just been told to stay off that ankle for at least two days.'

'I could do that in my own house! I'm sure no one will let me starve and Charlie said he would make me a crutch. Who do you think you are anyway?'

'My dear Sarah——' he pushed himself away from the door '—much as this obviously displeases you, you will stay here where Mrs Tibbs can look after you and, because we've had to declare a week's holiday from school, you can help *her* by entertaining Sally and Ben a bit. It's the most practical, sensible arrangement besides being what you will do because *I* say so and the sooner you get over your petty and ridiculous bout of emotion and bad temper the better. And don't bother to tell me I get around as if I own the place—I do.'

'I *wasn't*——' She broke off and bit her lip.

'Or something of that nature.'

She drew a shaky, exasperated breath, then discovered ridiculous tears misting her glasses again, so she pulled them off, wiped them on her blouse, wiped her nose with the back of her hand, and finally swore herself.

'I'm so glad Billy is not here to hear you,' Cliff said placidly. 'Feel better?'

'I just wish you'd go away!'

'OK—or you could have another cry on my shoulder.'

'I would never have done that if I hadn't had a hell of a morning on top of a sleepless night, if my ankle hadn't been aching, if you hadn't insulted me terribly and if I hadn't been feeling *guilty* about Billy Pascoe,' she said bitterly.

He sat down on the end of the bed and looked at her with a frown in his eyes. 'Why should you feel guilty about him?'

'I was a bit tough on him yesterday.' She grimaced bleakly. 'His mother thought that was why he hid like that.'

'Sarah, even from my limited experience of Billy Pascoe it's obvious you would need the patience of a saint to cope with him.'

'But that's just *it*,' she said frustratedly. 'Normally I do have the—well, not the patience of a saint but...a lot *more* patience than I seem to have at the moment.'

'So what do you attribute this sudden falling off in patience to?'

Sarah opened her mouth, shut it, couldn't look at him and finally muttered, 'Perhaps I need a break, that's all.'

'Then this is the solution,' he said after a long moment. 'Until the end of term at least when you could take a proper holiday. Sarah?'

She was forced to look up at him at last and although his expression was unreadable it was also narrowed and acute and she got the highly uncomfortable feeling that he understood only too well what the cause of her problems was. 'Yes...well, you could be right,' she said hastily. 'I...OK.'

Mrs Tibbs drew a bath for her and helped her to the bathroom then left her to soak away her woes for a while but it wasn't easy when one had on one's mind a series of thoughts that tended to go round in circles, when words and phrases like 'harem' and 'spinsterish little soul' seemed to be burnt into your consciousness, when, although you would have died rather than do it, the memory of crying into Cliff Wyatt's shoulder refused to be banished from your mind—not from the crying point of view but the safe, solid feel of it against your cheek and the tantalising, purely masculine scent that had assailed you . . .

But finally, clad in a fresh nightgown and in bed in the darkened guest bedroom with her ankle cradled on a pillow, she fell asleep deeply and dreamlessly and for hours.

It was Ben and Sally who finally woke her, coming ahead of Mrs Tibbs who brought a dinner-tray. She ate with surprising appetite, and was apprised of the fact that Uncle Cliff had had a lot of her things brought over, including Cindy Lawson's wedding-dress so she wouldn't have time to get bored, they said seriously.

Sarah grimaced. But it was hard not to be touched when the two children brought her their favourite jigsaw puzzle and Mrs Tibbs supplied a large tray and they started on it together, with solicitous care to make sure that when they hopped on the bed they didn't hurt her ankle.

It was Cliff who sent them to bed after about an hour, something they took in good part mostly, and Sarah couldn't help being further touched when they both gave her a hug as they said goodnight.

'How are you feeling?' their uncle asked as Mrs Tibbs took them off to have their baths. He was showered and changed and out of his cattleman mode in a pair of grey denims and a checked grey and white shirt beneath a sage-green V-necked pullover.

Sarah slid down against the pile of pillows and pulled the covers up. 'Fine. Thanks.'

'Now that can't be true,' he said with a slight smile. 'Don't forget the doctor gave you some pain-killers to help you through the next couple of days.'

'I . . . took one with dinner.'

'Good. What about your sunburn?' He came closer and inspected her small pink face on the pillows, surrounded by the loose, shining mass of chestnut hair which she'd washed in the bath and left to its own devices.

Sarah stared up at him rather owl-like through her glasses. 'Mrs Tibbs gave me some lanolin.'

'Good old lanolin,' he said wryly. 'So there's nothing I can get you—such as a good *stiff* brandy?'

She blinked and licked her lips. 'That mightn't go well with the pills.'

'No, of course not—thoughtless of me. What I had thought it might do was relax you sufficiently to make you think a little less darkly of me and—some of the things I said today.'

Sarah's eyes widened. 'Are you apologising?' she asked incredulously.

He pulled up a chair and sat down beside the bed. 'Why don't you tell me,' he said pensively, 'exactly what I should apologise for—and I'll try to oblige?'

Sarah nearly bit her tongue as the words rushed up. 'You don't think telling the whole world I was a frustrated spinster cherishing secret hopes of . . . of *you* deserves an apology? Or telling me to shut up in front of my entire school?'

His lips twisted. 'Well, I am sorry for telling you to shut up in front of your entire school. As for the other——'

But Sarah, who had gone from nearly biting her tongue unwittingly to wishing she had deliberately, said suddenly, wearily and desolately, 'Don't. Please. I . . . could we just leave it?'

He held her gaze with a frown in his own. Then he said in a different, even voice, 'But you know that's not going to solve anything, Sarah, don't you? Because I believe you're basically a very honest person who finds it hard not to say what you think, and so, within my limitations, am I. Which is to say, we can't go on circling each other like this; it's certainly not doing you any good.'

Sarah swallowed, wished herself on the other side of the continent as more heat flooded her already pink cheeks, and then sighed deeply, knowing that it was probably both futile and dishonest to pretend she didn't know what he meant. 'All right.' She hitched her pillows up so that she wasn't at quite such a disadvantage and smoothed the front of her unexceptional and modest nightgown down. She also moved her ankle to a more comfortable spot. Then she clasped her hands in front of her on the covers. 'This is one of those things that happens from time to time, I guess,' she said composedly.

'It happens to you often?' he queried quietly but with a sceptically lifted eyebrow.

Oh, God, she thought, why are you putting me through this?

'Perhaps that wasn't a good way to put it,' she said slowly but thinking furiously. 'What I mean is, I haven't got to this age without realising that rushing into these things is unwise to say the least and I think I've got this firm conviction within me now that when . . . a man comes along he has to be the *right* man; it has to be special and permanent and the most important thing in my life, and if it's not all those things I'm quite happy to stay the way I am—or was,' she added, and her blue eyes were completely honest if bleakly so as she raised them to his.

'I see,' he said slowly. 'But these things don't always happen that way, Sarah.'

She conceded this with a little gesture. 'On the other hand, I have this equally firm conviction that, having reached twenty-six and all this maturity and wisdom——' she grimaced '—to throw it away on someone like you, whom I barely know and whom, if you'll forgive me, I have to cherish the gravest doubts about from, well, *that* point of view, would be a piece of supreme folly on my part.'

'I'm glad you stressed *that* point of view,' he said gravely. 'It makes it just short of a total character assassination, for which I'm humbly grateful.'

To her amazement, as she observed the wicked little glint of amusement in his dark eyes, Sarah found herself half smiling. 'You know what I mean.'

'You mean that unless I make all the motions of a man intent on wooing and winning you with a view to wedlock you're not even prepared to consider me,' he said.

'Now that does sound like *Pride and Prejudice*,' she retorted, no longer smiling.

'But true nevertheless.'

'Had it crossed your mind?'

'No, Sarah, it hadn't,' he said calmly. 'Although I must say it occurred to me that when you weren't fighting me you were a rather peaceful, well-organised——'

'You've told me that before,' she broke in with considerable irony.

'And you replied that you'd rather die than be married for your domesticity,' he replied reminiscently.

For some reason she blushed and as a consequence said tartly, 'I haven't changed my mind!' And added briskly, 'So, now we've had it all out and got it settled, perhaps we could get on with our lives in some sort of harmony?'

His dark eyes lingered on her thoughtfully until finally he smiled enigmatically. 'Well, we can try.' He stood up. 'What would you like to do now?'

'Go to sleep, I guess,' she said and hoped it didn't sound as forlorn to him as it had to her so she added exasperatedly, 'I don't have a lot of options at the moment, do I?'

'I just thought you might like to cast around for some other problem you could bend your mind to and settle per the sole medium of intellect.'

Her eyes widened as the import of his words sank in. Then she said through her teeth, 'Go away, please. Why is it that when women try to be rational and reasonable about these things men always object?'

'I can't answer for the world of men at large but in this case it could be because this man knows there are some things that aren't always susceptible to reason and rationality. There, that's a thought for you take to sleep with you, Miss Sutherland. Goodnight. I do hope your ankle doesn't bother you through the night.' And with this parting shot, delivered so politely despite its impact being somewhat like a missile landing, as he very well knew, she thought darkly, he took himself off.

She stared at the closed door and took several deep breaths.

CHAPTER FOUR

THANKFULLY, Sarah was spared Cliff Wyatt's presence for the next four days. He went back to supervise the muster so she was able to work on her resolve to put all thoughts of him in one context, out of mind, but— not that she'd expected it to be easy—it proved terribly hard.

She thought it might have something to do with being in his house, she suspected it might have a lot to do with Mrs Tibbs, who, for reasons best known to herself, took to deferring to her as if she were in charge of the household, causing Sarah to flinch inwardly and fume yet again over the way Cliff Wyatt had told the whole world that she cherished a secret desire to be made off with to his harem. I might have known everyone would pick *that* one up, she thought gloomily several times. But surely Mrs Tibbs doesn't seriously believe I...? Her thoughts had the awkward habit of trailing off uncertainly at that point, however.

So far as being in his house went, and even despite the fact that she could only hobble about on the crutch Charlie had fashioned for her and not even do a lot of that for the first two days, she found herself curiously fascinated by it. By the fact that it had been furnished well but had an impersonal air about it. It's such a lovely old house, it deserves better, she mused once. I wonder why Wendy and Amy didn't do something about it? Well, Wendy, anyway, she amended her thoughts, because she'd also come to the con-

clusion that despite Cliff Wyatt's disclaimer of anything formal between them Wendy had other ideas.
And, to make matters worse, Mrs Tibbs took it upon
herself that day to show her cupboards full of crystal,
silver and linen, vases, ornaments, lamps, even
paintings stacked away and unpacked as yet.

'Needs a woman's touch, this place,' Mrs Tibbs said
with what seemed to Sarah to be elaborate casualness.

'I...this is a bit surprising,' Sarah heard herself
reply. 'I mean, I would have thought that once he got
Edgeleigh back on its feet he'd...well, everyone says
Coorilla is their home base.'

Mrs Tibbs snorted. 'What's that thing about best-
laid plans? See, the plan was for Coorilla to be turned
over to that silly Amy and her husband to run and
make their home while Cliff lived here, but, now she's
done the flit, things have got themselves unplanned,
you might say.'

'I see.'

'Quite thought Miss Green-eyes would make it her
business to get in among all this stuff but Cliff didn't
give her any encouragement,' Mrs Tibbs said with a
swift, significant glance in Sarah's direction.

'So do you think you're wrong about her?' Sarah
asked slowly, hating herself a bit for fishing in this
manner but not able to help herself.

'No way! She's got him firmly in her sights all right.
Whether he wants to be there is another matter.'

'Because he didn't encourage her to...?' Sarah
waved an eloquent hand.

Mrs Tibbs grimaced but mainly, Sarah realised, because she was battling with the dilemma of whether
to be honest or to continue encouraging her as she
seemed to have made it her mission. 'Well, what he

said was, actually, that until they worked out what the hell was going to happen with Amy they should leave it all be. But mark my words, Sarah, Miss Wendy Wilson isn't going to find it such an easy job to nail Cliff Wyatt!'

'Oh, well, it's got nothing to do with me,' Sarah murmured and turned away.

Mrs Tibbs snorted again.

But one thing stayed in Sarah's mind apart from the obvious—that if Cliff Wyatt intended to remain a bachelor it was going to be a particularly fine bachelor establishment when everything out of those cupboards was deployed about the homestead.

But during those four days she mainly concentrated on getting over her disability and on keeping Sally and Ben happy and occupied. And the only time she gave rein to her feelings about the house was on the afternoon of the fourth day when she found four lovely pink roses in the rather wild, abandoned garden so picked them and went in search of a vase for them.

But it was that evening after the children were in bed and when she was in the lounge, standing in a pool of light with the rest of the room shadowy around her, readjusting her roses in their silver vase, that Cliff came home.

They'd not expected him because word had filtered through that the muster party would not be back until the following morning, but nevertheless something alerted her and she glanced up to see him standing in the doorway only a few feet from her, regarding her expressionlessly but with a curiously arrogant tilt to his head.

She took her hands from the blooms as if she'd suddenly been burnt, put some unwise pressure on her ankle and had to lean heavily on her crutch to stay upright. 'I didn't hear you!' she said uncertainly.

'So I gathered.' His tone was clipped, his voice cool as he allowed his dark gaze to drift over her. She was wearing a gathered navy blue skirt with little white polka dots, a fluffy white angora sweater she'd knitted herself and her hair was tied back with a navy ribbon.

'We didn't expect you until tomorrow,' she said then, trying to match his cool tone. 'Has there been a problem?'

When he answered, after a curiously tense little pause, he said, 'Yes. A clogged fuel line on the chopper so I drove back—you must have been pretty deep in thought not to hear the Land Rover.'

Sarah blinked through her glasses as she realised that she must have indeed. 'I...yes,' she said huskily. She had the distinct feeling that it wasn't only a clogged fuel line that was annoying him but something she'd done as well; although she knew full well why *she* had reacted so precipitately she only prayed that wasn't it, and she took refuge in politeness. 'I think Mrs Tibbs has gone to bed—can I get you something to eat? You look tired and irritable.'

'I am tired and irritable.' He raked a hand through his dusty dark hair.

'Then——'

'Yes, Sarah, you may,' he said curtly. 'Just some coffee and a snack; I'm driving back shortly.' And he wheeled about and disappeared towards his bedroom.

For a moment, Sarah stayed where she was with her hand to her mouth and a wary, desolate look in her eyes, then she limped towards the kitchen.

*   *   *

'Thank you.' Cliff finished the last of the toasted chicken sandwiches she'd made and drank his coffee. 'How's everything here?' he added abruptly.

'Fine. Sally and Ben are happy, Amy has rung every day and—everything's fine,' she repeated.

'What about you?'

'I'm almost as good as new.'

'When you got such a shock to see me, it didn't quite look like that. In fact it looked as if your ankle is still pretty sore.' He said it roughly as if it was a further source of annoyance to him.

'If it is I don't know why it should be aggravating you to this extent,' she said very quietly and poured him another cup of coffee.

'Then I'll tell you,' he said precisely. 'You looked— before you were aware of my existence—like the warm, peaceful chatelaine of this establishment, deep in thought certainly but in tune with your surroundings and happy to be so.'

Sarah closed her eyes because her prayers had not been answered. In the moments before she'd looked up and seen him, that was exactly what had happened to her; the tight rein on her emotions had eluded her briefly and she'd given herself over to the pleasure of four roses in a lovely room and a lovely house, and that was, of course, why she'd reacted so guiltily.

'And that,' he continued, 'for some reason or other, made me remember how much you enjoyed kissing me, Sarah, and how much I'd like to be doing something along those lines with you rather than driving twenty miles back to the camp along a hell of a road in the middle of the night with a bloody tool that we should never have been without anyway. Strange, isn't it?' he said mockingly and sat back with his arms

folded over the bulky charcoal sweater he'd added to
his khaki shirt and trousers.

'Yes, it is,' she answered in a pained voice, 'since
I'm not the chatelaine and that wasn't quite how I
saw myself——'

'How much of a leap forward in your imagination
would it take to make the adjustment?' he asked with
a sardonic lift of an eyebrow.

'Stop it,' she whispered, standing up unsteadily.
'I'm only here because it was your idea; *I* knew it was
not what I should do to——' She stopped abruptly.

'Do to yourself?' he suggested, and added drily,
'Or me for that matter. So I'm beginning to agree
with you, Sarah.'

'This is an . . . impossible situation.'

'Oh, definitely. What do *you* suggest, as a matter
of interest?'

She straightened her spine. 'Look, you can't
seriously expect me to believe you want to have anything other than a brief affair with me and I even find
that hard to believe——'

'There's one way to prove that.'

'Well, I'm not going to do it,' she said with angry
colour pouring into her cheeks.

He got up. 'You know, you shouldn't base your
estimation of my taste in women entirely on Wendy,
Sarah. Because it so happens that I'm fully aware that
there is more to it than a glossy, glamorous, well-
packaged exterior.'

'But I just don't have any gloss or glamour——'
She broke off and bit her lip.

'You have a way of kissing, however, that is unexpectedly—satisfying,' he drawled. 'And you have a

neat, slender little figure that is unexpectedly
tantalising.'

'Have you *any* idea how that one word "unexpectedly" gives you away, Mr Wyatt?' she said
through her teeth. 'If not I'll tell you what it does to
me—it makes me quite sure you're no better than a
tom cat on the prowl because he's stuck out here
without his unusual ... resources!'

He came round the table leisurely, sat on the corner
and put his fingers meditatively beneath her chin,
tilting it up gently. 'That's a very black picture you
paint of me, Sarah, and not quite an accurate one. I
have had one—resource, as you put it, barely gone
from my side, had I wanted to. But I'm a little allergic
to...' he paused ' ... being manipulated into certain
things as well as quite allergic to brazen attempts to
share my bed; but I wonder if you know all that,' he
mused, 'and have planned a much more subtle
approach?'

Sarah gasped but the arrogant tilt of his head was
all too clearly printed in her memory. 'You
thought ... is *that* what you thought when you came
home?'

'It crossed my mind,' he agreed. 'Unfortunately in
some respects I am the—reprehensible person you take
me for.' He smiled without compunction. 'But I tend,
on reflection, to discount that now. And I think I can
honestly say to you that I am, however unexpectedly,
attracted by quite a few things in you, Sarah
Sutherland. Your fighting nature——' he smiled again
wryly '—and the very pleasant experience it turned
out to be when I kissed you against your will,
the——' his gaze moved fleetingly downwards then
back to her wide, stunned eyes '—feeling I have, which

incidentally has been intensified by finally seeing you out of your everlasting jeans and shirt, that there's a delicate but shapely body underneath it all with small but sweet, crushed-velvet-tipped breasts, a tiny waist and possibly——'

The slap of her hand against his cheekbone sounded unnaturally loud in the quiet house. But although Cliff Wyatt winced briefly he also laughed softly and immediately put his hands on her waist, imprisoning her as he said, 'I knew we'd get around to that one day! I suppose I should just be thankful you didn't punch me in the mouth as you offered to do after we'd barely met. But if you think I don't realise that's an invitation to—respond, as *I* once postulated, think again, Sarah.'

'No——'

'You've said that before too,' he drawled.

But Sarah by this time was trembling down the length of her with a mixture of fury and fright which caused him to narrow his eyes as he felt it through his hands, before she said in a low, intense voice, 'Don't play games with me, Cliff Wyatt. I'm not a child and I'm not a flirt and the fact that you're a good-looking cynic who gets pursued by brazen women, which I think is what you were trying to tell me, doesn't impress me in the slightest, nor do your insults—and that's all I meant to show you!'

He didn't bother to deny the charge; he simply raised an eyebrow and said, 'If I am, aren't you?'

'A cynic?' she said uncertainly.

'I thought that was what you were trying to tell me when you delivered that long sermon on the night you sprained your ankle? That you were done with all

casual encounters and, if the big show didn't turn up
for you, too bad. Or something to that effect.'

'I don't see how you can call that cynical; it's the
opposite if anything,' she countered.

'But you took one look at me and became extremely cynical, I would have thought.'

'Because you... *deserve* it,' Sarah said frustratedly.

'Why? On account of kissing a girl who didn't
happen to be you on the veranda one night?' he
queried blandly.

'Oh! Will you let me go?' Sarah commanded
fiercely.

'Certainly,' he replied, and did so promptly
although he had to steady her while she felt for her
crutch. 'Do you get the feeling,' he added politely,
'that we're still going round and round in rather futile
circles, Sarah?'

'*Yes*.' She bit her lip. 'But because you're pro-
moting them,' she added bitterly.

'I'm also, so I'm told, a hard man to say no to,'
he said sweetly.

'Of *all* the ... !'

He laughed and got up off the table. 'The other
thing I am, unfortunately, is a man pressed for time
at the moment. If I don't get back soon, we won't
get the chopper ready by morning and this blasted,
I'm tempted to think even cursed, muster will drag
on yet another day. So I'll say farewell in the
meantime, Miss Sutherland, and hope to see you
tomorrow.'

'No, you won't, not here!' And she turned away
and presented a furious, straight back to him.

He only laughed softly and walked out.

* * *

But she was there when he got back late in the afternoon of the next day and she was concerned and anxious enough to be able to put aside some things as she answered his highly mocking, ironic look when they first met.

'It's Sally and Ben,' she said straightly. 'As well as Billy Pascoe and one other kid. We think they've got chicken-pox.'

They were in his study where she'd come to seek him out and he sat down at the oak desk and said savagely, 'Bloody hell! Does it never end? How on earth did they pick it up here of all places?'

'I've worked that out. One of the kids had a friend to stay for a couple of days. Apparently he broke out as soon as he got home and the incubation period fits in—he came to school and played with the lot of them so we can expect every child in the place who hasn't had chicken-pox to get it, I would imagine.'

Cliff swore wearily. 'Well, we'll just have to declare a further holiday. Are they very sick?'

'They're fractious and uncomfortable but as far as the chicken-pox goes it's not a terribly serious disease, it's just, well, Sally wants her mother——' She stopped awkwardly.

'What?'

'And Ben, for the first time, wants to know what's happened to his father and he's quite truculent about it. I must say I wondered about that.'

'What about it?'

'How you'd handled their father's disappearance out of their lives. Why they never mentioned him, that kind of thing, but it's none of my business so I——'

'We told them he'd had to go away on business,' Cliff said curtly. 'Whether they believed it, seeing their mother so abject and miserable all the time, remained to be seen, which I pointed out to Amy, but to be honest I couldn't think what else to do. I also, I suppose, was living in the hope,' he added bitingly, 'that this whole stupid mess would clear itself up *before* they began to worry too much.'

Sarah grimaced.

'And I'm quite sure you're about to tell me you should always be honest with children—although not about Father Christmas,' he said with all the arrogance he was capable of.

'No, I wasn't,' Sarah replied quietly.

'You surprise me,' he said coldly.

'Well, for one thing I wouldn't presume to, not with you in this mood at least,' she said calmly. 'But I think we can take it as read now that they were concerned, or Ben was but he buried it at the back of his mind because he didn't know how to cope with it, but now that he's feeling sick and sorry for himself it's all boiled up.'

Cliff made an abrupt movement. 'I'll get on the phone to Amy. Look, don't make them any promises until I've spoken to her—I take it you've decided to put aside your spinsterish prejudices against me for the time being?' he said with a suddenly sardonic look.

'If you mean will I help two sick, unhappy kids out until their mother comes, yes, I will,' she responded evenly, and couldn't help adding, 'Which is a lot more than you deserve, incidentally.'

He looked into the deep blue of her eyes behind her glasses, smiled a tigerish little smile and murmured, 'Yes, ma'am. Thank you, ma'am.'

*   *   *

He didn't tell her the result of his call to Amy until they were having dinner together, alone.

'Mrs Tibbs,' Sarah had said when she'd realised that good lady's plan for a tête-à-tête dinner, 'don't do this to me—what I mean is,' she'd changed tack hastily, 'I would rather eat with you.'

'Too late now,' Mrs Tibbs had said laconically. 'I ate my dinner the same time the kids had theirs and you were having a break and a bath. I also asked the boss if this was OK.' She'd gestured to the small table she'd set in the breakfast-room with, Sarah noticed, some of the finery from the cupboards. 'He said fine. He also told me he was looking forward to something a bit different from the hash the camp cook dished up so I done you some lamb cutlets with soup before and a trifle after. Be ready in about two minutes.'

Sarah had sighed helplessly. 'Well, I'll go and check on the kids.'

'They're asleep. Cliff read to 'em and settled 'em down no end but I'll keep an ear open while you have your dinner. Here.' And she'd handed Sarah a bottle of wine and a corkscrew. 'Thought this might go well.'

And that was how Cliff Wyatt came to find her turning a bottle of wine round in her hands as he entered the room. 'Now that's a good idea,' he said casually.

'It wasn't mine.' Sarah put the wine down.

'None the same it was mine; you look as if you could do with a bit of a lift,' Mrs Tibbs remarked as she pushed in a trolley laden with covered dishes. 'I'll leave you two to it!'

'What a character,' Cliff said with a grin when the door was safely closed. 'Such a rough diamond yet able to come up with all this.' He waved a hand at the elegant table. 'And this,' he added appreciatively, lifting some covers.

'Yes.'

He looked her over. 'Sit down, Sarah. You do look a bit—taxed.'

She glanced at him expressionlessly and did as she was bid. He'd showered and changed into brown corduroy trousers and a fine cream wool sweater. She was wearing the same ensemble she'd had on the night before. And she was quite silent as he served the soup—creamy pumpkin with little florets of cauliflower floating in it—and opened the wine.

'Cheers,' he said, sitting at last. 'I couldn't get hold of Amy.'

Her eyes widened.

'Tonight, that is,' he added, and started on his soup. 'Believe it or not she and Ross are on their way to an island in the Whitsundays to try to sort things out between them. It would appear that he stormed the bastion today, according to Wendy, and told Amy that the least she could do was listen to him.'

'Well, that's good news, isn't it?' Sarah said cautiously.

'Of course. But it does pose the question of whether I should interrupt them and no doubt throw Amy into a panic over a routine childhood ailment or give them a few days' peace.'

Sarah finished her soup before she said, 'If you feel you can set Sally and Ben's minds at rest, why not give them a few days' peace?'

'I might need your help, though.'

'I told you I would.'

He got up to serve the cutlets. 'I thought you might like to tack on an addendum. Provided you behave yourself, Mr Wyatt, sort of thing.' He handed her her plate with perfect courtesy and topped up her wine before sitting down himself again.

A fighting little glint entered Sarah's eye although she said composedly, 'I'm never one to waste time hitting my head against a brick wall—Mr Wyatt. But I can't help wondering if I've wounded your vanity severely.'

'Oh? Why is that?'

'Because of the way you keep returning to the subject, as if you didn't know,' she retorted.

He smiled sweetly at her and raised his glass in a silent toast. 'OK. I suppose you have.'

This was the last thing Sarah was expecting and she nearly choked on a mouthful of peas.

'Have some wine,' he advised.

She flashed him a speaking look but took several sips.

'Better? Good. Sarah, if the truth be told,' he said meditatively, 'I can't work out if you're too good to be true or if you're a thorn sent expressly to lodge in my side, so, as a way to solve the mystery as well as to solve *our* dilemma, why don't you tell me some more about you? Did you arrive in this world as a model of wisdom and common sense, albeit a short-sighted one? Or is the way you are now a backlash against a wild and wanton youth or some deeply unhappy affair or some trauma to do with your parents? Those kind of things,' he finished conversationally.

'Do I look as if I spent a wild and wanton youth?' she said acidly.

'Not at all but looks can be so deceiving. For example——'

'If you're going to refer to how I kissed you again,' she said hastily and swallowed some more wine, 'I'm sick to death of hearing about it. You . . . took me by surprise; you obviously know a great deal about it, including *how* to take unsuspecting females by surprise and turn it to your advantage!'

He said nothing but his gaze never wavered from her face until she breathed exasperatedly, took her glasses off, polished them agitatedly on the table-cloth, and finally said shortly, 'All right, that's not quite true but what *is* true is not so flattering to you either, you know.'

'What's that?' he murmured.

'That I'm suffering from a case of . . . to use your terms, spinster's blues——' she grimaced '—and it caught me unawares. That's all. Perhaps I ought to take something you said to me once to heart and . . . get to know Tim Markwell better.'

But there came a look of such amusement to his eyes that her hands trembled and she put them out of sight below the table suddenly. 'Yes, why don't you give it a try?' he said blandly. 'I'd be interested to hear the result.'

She swallowed. 'Look here——'

But he laughed softly. 'You're right, enough of this—is that what you were going to say? Well, I'm in agreement. What else would you like to talk about?'

'Nothing.'

'Now, Sarah, don't sulk,' he chided gravely. 'There was something else I wanted to talk to you about as a matter of fact—young Donald Lawson.'

Sarah looked up, arrested, her eyes wide and blue with surprise. 'What about him?'

'Since you mentioned how bright and brainy he is, I've taken a bit of time to get to know him, and you're right again,' he said wryly. 'He deserves better. So I took the opportunity to—sound out the subject with Jim. He has agreed, at the end of this term, to Donald's going to live at Coorilla with a family who've lived and worked on the property for years and I know well, so that he'll be able to go to a proper high school—Coorilla's only an hour or so by bus from Toowoomba and there is a school bus that passes the gates.'

'Oh!' Sarah closed her eyes but they flew open immediately, 'Oh, I can't thank you enough—this is *marvellous*!'

He regarded her enigmatically. 'It could mean a bit more work for you, though. I should imagine he'll need some extra preparation.'

'I'll only be too happy to do it,' Sarah said earnestly. 'Have you told Donald? I think it will come as such a relief to him; I think he was getting really frustrated—he'll be fourteen in a couple of weeks and . . .' She waved a hand expressively.

'No, I'll let his father do that. I think Jim was secretly relieved although, as you so rightly observed, he's still a bit dazed at having produced such a brainy kid. But with Cindy's wedding approaching, apparently the Lawson household is becoming such a turbulent place, he was rather at his wits' end.'

Sarah laughed. 'She's exhibiting all the usual symptoms of a bride-to-be. Only yesterday she told me that if she could change her mind and have a slim, slinky dress she's decided that's what she really wants. I didn't remind her that I'd suggested something a little less ornate originally.'

Cliff looked at her with comic dread. 'Heaven's above, don't tell me you're going to change it!'

'I couldn't. I'd have to start all over again and the wedding's only about a month away. No, I hope I managed to persuade her it'll be fine.'

'You're a braver soul than I am, Gunga Din,' he murmured. 'Well, shall we try Mrs Tibbs' trifle?'

They ate the rest of the meal companionably, although Sarah was tempted to pinch herself a couple of times, but she was in such a genuine glow about Donald's good fate, she didn't find it that hard to respond to his conversation. Nor did he introduce anything controversial.

And at the end of it, when she stood up to clear away and he said he had some work to do, she said naturally, 'I don't want to bore you with too much gratitude, but it's a *very* good thing you've done for Donald Lawson.'

He lay back in his chair and his dark eyes were quizzical as they roamed over her briefly. Then he stood up and said formally, 'Thank you for those kind words, Miss Sutherland. I suspect I'll cherish them.'

But, before Sarah could think of anything to say in return, he strolled out of the breakfast-room.

The next few days continued in kind.

Sally and Ben got over the worst symptoms of their chicken-pox and an old-fashioned remedy of Mrs Tibbs' stopped them from feeling too itchy.

Cliff got hold of Amy and assured her she had absolutely nothing to worry about, the kids were fine, which was only a slight deviation from the truth, he told Sarah, and told Amy not to worry about ringing in daily. In fact, as much due to his efforts as to

Sarah's and Mrs Tibbs', Sally and Ben soon returned
to their state of mental well-being.

'I'm amazed how good he is with them,' Sarah remarked, unwisely as it turned out, to Mrs Tibbs once.

'Which just goes to show how good he'd be with
his own kids,' that good lady replied. 'Thought of
that, Sarah?'

'*No*. Why should I?' Sarah countered irately.

'It's always a good idea to think of these things,'
Mrs Tibbs said airily, and went on her way.

Sarah glared after her but it was that same
afternoon that she had it further demonstrated to her
what a paragon a lot of people thought Cliff Wyatt
was.

Cindy and Jean Lawson came up for a fitting of
the wedding-dress and they were in the sewing-room
next to the study which Mrs Tibbs had suggested Sarah
use "seeing as that's what it's purpose in life is", and
Jean was still on cloud nine about Donald.

'But that's why he's such a good boss and why he'll
get this place going if it kills him, Jim reckons,' she
said glowingly.

Cindy was in the wedding-dress and Sarah was
kneeling on the floor in front of her, attempting to
pin up the hem. 'Because of Donald?' she queried a
bit indistinctly with a couple of pins in her mouth.
'Cindy, could you just stand still for a moment?'

'Not only Donald but that's a real part of it!' Jean
enthused. 'But he also does so much; there's nothing
going on he doesn't know about and he can turn his
hand to anything he expects the blokes to do. Look
how he camped out with them on the muster! And
Jim reckons he can shoe a horse as well as the black-
smith, he can ride as good as any of them, as well as

being able to fly that helicopter and fix it when it goes wrong. He's like a different person when he's working and although he can be tough he can be like one of them too.'

'I've noticed that—Cindy!'

'I want to *see* myself, Sarah,' Cindy said petulantly.

'All in good time.'

'And then on top of it all,' Jean continued unperturbed, 'he takes this *interest* in us and our families. Why, he even told Cindy he'd love to come to the wedding!'

'He did too!' Cindy said, sounding momentarily diverted from whatever was ailing her. 'I think he's a lovely man. I just . . .' She stopped and sighed. 'I'm just not sure about this dress now.'

Sarah and Jean glanced at each other expressively. 'But it's exactly what you wanted, love!' Jean said beguilingly. 'And after all the trouble Sarah's been to!'

'There.' Sarah sat on the floor. 'Now we need a mirror. I'm sure Cliff wouldn't mind if I took you through to the master bedroom—it's the only full-length mirror I can think of. Just go carefully Cindy, and lift the skirt up a little.'

And that was how it was that as they were crossing the long central passageway Cliff Wyatt came unexpectedly out of the study, stopped dead, then said, 'Why, Cindy—you look absolutely *stunning*!'

The metamorphosis this achieved was remarkable. Sarah saw Cindy's cross, woebegone little face light up like a candle as she said breathlessly, 'Do you really think so, Mr Wyatt?'

'I think,' he said gravely, 'you're one of the prettiest brides I've ever seen.'

*   *   *

'I believe I owe you another debt of gratitude,' Sarah said over dinner for two that night—something she hadn't been able to cure Mrs Tibbs of providing. 'But I didn't expect you to perjure your soul.'

He looked amused. 'If we're talking about Cindy, I didn't exactly.'

'No?' Sarah looked across at him wryly. 'I was under the impression that her dress didn't appeal to you in the slightest.'

'All the same,' he responded lazily, 'it is stunning. And for a couple of moments she looked so happy and radiant, *she* was quite stunning. Besides which, I thought it was time someone took a stand.'

'Did you——?' Sarah narrowed her eyes as she suddenly remembered that the sewing-room was next door to his study. 'Did you hear... what we were talking about this afternoon?'

'Some of it,' he said innocently. 'Your window was open and so was mine—and they are right next door to each other.'

'So that's...I'm surprised you haven't got a swollen head,' she said severely. 'You could have closed your window!'

His eyes laughed at her. 'But then I might not have been in the position to solve the problem of the dress.'

'No,' Sarah said gloomily.

'I really thought that would appeal to you,' he mused quizzically.

'It does. I'm merely ruminating on the nature of certain things.'

'Such as?'

'How, after one word from you, Cindy is convinced she was right all along in her choice of dress, indeed will cherish that dress for the rest of her life, is a transformed girl, you might even say—it just doesn't seem quite fair.'

'I would concentrate on the fact that I saw the opportunity to do you a good turn, and took it,' he recommended.

'I will,' she promised. 'Well, by tomorrow morning I'm sure I'll have persuaded myself to see it exactly in that light.'

His lips twisted. 'And for the rest of tonight?'

Sarah opened her mouth, closed it, felt the colour mounting in her cheeks and said expressionlessly, 'I was only joking.'

'Of course.'

It occurred to her as she lay in bed that night, unable to get to sleep, that she was in a minority of one regarding her employer... And even that's getting harder and harder to be, she thought unhappily, setting aside, of course, the awful irony of... well, say it, Sarah...how much he attracts you despite your better judgement. If only Amy and Ross would come home and claim their children! Then I wouldn't have to put up with living side by side with him.

'Put up with it?' she whispered to herself and smiled a bitter little smile at the ceiling. 'Going away from here, even back to my cottage, is going to be like going back to a half-life, like turning off the sun ... If I had any sense, I'd get right away from Edgeleigh. But who would help Donald then? And who would have the patience to at least *try* and get through to Billy Pascoe?'

CHAPTER FIVE

SARAH was heavy-eyed and slow the next morning, something that didn't go unnoticed by her employer who, with his customary vigour, had turned his attention to the homestead garden and enlisted her advice, saying that for someone who grew as many things in pots as she did she must have some ideas. And the only reason she'd not got herself out of it somehow had been because it was the first time Sally and Ben were to be allowed outside and they'd begged her to go too.

'Is your ankle still playing up?' he demanded with a tinge of impatience. 'Why didn't you say so?'

'It's not,' she replied quietly. 'I only get a faint twinge now and then.'

'So?' he queried autocratically, his dark eyes acute and bright—in fact everything about him, in his brown cords and a dark green sweater against the lovely fresh morning air, was lean, fit, dynamic and enough to make her catch her breath unwittingly.

'I . . . it's nothing,' she said helplessly. 'Uh—these roses could do with a heavy pruning but July is the best month for that when they're all but dormant.'

'Do you list pruning roses bushes as one of your accomplishments, Sarah? Your *many* accomplishments?'

She decided to ignore the subtle mockery in his voice because she wasn't sure why it should have returned after being absent for the last few days, and tried to

ignore the little shaft of pain that pierced her heart.
'Yes, I've pruned a few rose bushes,' she said steadily.
'I did once think of becoming a horticulturalist.'

'Then why are you so reluctant to give me the ben-
efit of your advice? I would have thought this garden
and its reclamation would be an irresistible challenge
to a horticulturalist.'

She looked at him briefly. 'I'm not reluctant—I
didn't sleep very well last night, that's all.'

'Any special reason for that?'

'No. Sally and Ben are loving this.' She gazed
towards the two children playing like puppies on the
grass.

'End of subject, I gather. Yes, they are,' he said
drily. 'I think we'll leave this to another day.'

'No!' Sarah said involuntarily. 'I mean, we might
as well . . .' She bit her lip.

'Get it over and done with?' he supplied. 'You've
said that to me before too, although in that case we
never did get around to it.'

She swallowed and knew she was incapable of
crossing swords with him in this mood so she took a
deep breath and said, 'All right, yes, I must admit
that ever since I've been here I've been dying to, well,
get my hands on this garden.' And in cool, composed
tones that she dragged up somehow or other she went
on to tell him her ideas, finishing by saying, 'But it
would need a couple of strong men and a lot of water.'

'I've got plenty of strong men,' he commented.
'And it wouldn't be such a task to divert another line
from the bore.'

'There you go, then—I think Sally and Ben are
starting to flag; I'll take them in.'

'Why not?' he drawled.

As she turned away, she found to her horror that she had tears pricking her eyelids.

It got worse later the next day.

The fine weather abated and a cold westerly wind sprang up and blew with a vengeance, covering everything with eye-stinging red dust and giving both humans and animals alike the "willies", as Mrs Tibbs put it. And, although Sarah and the children remained in doors all day, the howling of the wind around the house was enough to set their nerves on edge and by late afternoon Ben and Sally were fractious, irritable and naughty and Sarah was beginning to feel as if she'd been run through a mangle.

It was not a good time to tangle with Cliff once again, she discovered, when she finally ran out of patience and confined the children to their room with the warning that they behave or else!

'Or else?' Cliff drawled, meeting her and barring her way in the passage as she closed their door with a snap.

'So?' she countered irately.

'It just seems rather imprecise, done in the heat of the moment and contrary to accepted how-to-deal-with-children practices, I would imagine—not what you would expect from such an avowed teacher and educator,' he explained with a curiously insolent glance from his dark eyes.

Sarah gritted her teeth. 'I'm not teaching them anything at the moment. I'm shut up with them in these appalling conditions—if I were their mother, I would have been a lot more precise about it, probably.'

'You mean you would have smacked them both and sent them to bed without dinner?' he suggested.

She bit her lip because she'd actually itched to do just that briefly.

He laughed softly. 'Dear me, Sarah, you do need a break but in fact I find it refreshingly human in you. It's just a pity it doesn't extend to—other areas of your life.'

Sarah eyed him angrily. She knew he'd been out battling the elements but he'd showered and changed and was wearing thick cords and a black jumper and he radiated a sort of sardonic vitality. Which caused her to say tartly, 'I've no idea what you mean but I also have no intention of being enlightened so don't waste your time, Mr Wyatt. May I get past?'

'In a moment,' he murmured. 'I'm not so easy to dismiss as two naughty kids, Miss Sutherland. I'm also your employer——'

'If you think that has the slightest bearing with me at the moment, you're wrong,' she flashed.

But he only laughed softly and took her wrist in one hand before she had the wit to realise what he was doing. 'Well, then I'll just have to fall back on the fact that I'm a lot bigger than you, won't I?'

'*You*...let me go,' she whispered and tried to break his grip but it was useless.

'It never ceases to amaze me how much sheer dynamite is packed into your petite frame, Sarah,' he marvelled. 'And no, I'm not going to let you go until I've had my say. Which is this——'

'If it's to do with my inhumanity—I think I can guess——'

'Well, that's just it, I think you can,' he said drily. 'And that's why you're so cross.' His lips twitched. 'But to my mind there would be one infallible way of ridding ourselves of the frustrations of a day like today. We could hand the kids over to Mrs Tibbs, we could repair to some private place such as my bedroom, build up the fire, close the curtains and you could allow me to take your clothes off one item at a time—you could even respond in kind if you were so moved—and I guarantee that what would follow would blot out the wind, naughty kids—and all your frustrations.'

'You . . . you . . .'

He watched her as she sought for words and failed. Then he said ingenuously, 'I do believe I've struck you speechless, Sarah Sutherland!'

She blinked several times then said hoarsely and unwisely, 'Why are you doing this? Why can't you just . . . leave me alone?'

'You know why, Sarah.' He released her wrist abruptly.

She rubbed it unthinkingly and he picked it up again and inspected the faint red marks on it. 'Sorry,' he said absently. 'I didn't mean to hurt you.'

She took a deep, trembling breath then, as he let her wrist go for the second time, she fled past him.

But, once in the safety of her bedroom, she covered her face with her hands as she leant against the door and tried to block out not the anger or feeling of being ill-used she should be burning with, but those insidious images he'd created, of them together creating an oasis of peace and warmth, of . . .

'No,' she whispered. 'Give me the strength to resist this. Why's it *so* hard?' she asked herself passionately then took her hands away and went to sit desolately on her bed.

'Because he attracts you as you've never been attracted before and it's no good telling yourself he *shouldn't*, that he's diabolically clever—and all the rest of it!' she muttered impatiently, and swallowed. Because the truth of the matter was, she also liked Cliff Wyatt when he wasn't being impossible, liked, admired . . . And am I just as much star-struck if not more so than everyone else in this wretched place? she thought and shivered. So what to do?

She got up and paced the room distractedly, hugging herself protectively. I don't think I can take much more but I don't know what to do . . .

What she did eventually, as a temporary measure, was to tell Mrs Tibbs she had a headache and wouldn't have dinner that night but just take a snack to eat in her room. Thus she saw no more of him that wild, windy day. But by dinnertime that night she knew she couldn't hide from him any longer and she hoped that by the time they did have dinner together she would have preached enough common sense to herself to take care of all eventualities. As it turned out she couldn't have been more wrong . . .

It was after dinner when Mrs Tibbs had served coffee in the lounge that she said carefully, 'Any idea how Amy is getting on?'

'Not a one. Why?' And he cast her a cool, indifferent glance.

Now don't get angry, Sarah, she warned herself. Why shouldn't I wonder when she's coming back or *if* she's coming back? She said evenly, 'Because now that Sally and Ben are so much better I was thinking of going back to my house, and starting up school again. And I ought to be spending more time with Donald——'

'Sarah.'

She'd been pouring the coffee but after a moment she turned to find him standing beside the fireplace with his hands shoved into his pocket and a sort of savage impatience written all over him.

'*What*?' she said huskily.

'You know damned well.'

'I know you've been trying to start a fight with me for days but I'm equally determined you won't succeed any more.'

'*Start* a fight?' He raised an ironic eyebrow at her. 'My dear Sarah, it's been a fight ever since we laid eyes on each other.'

'Not of my choice, it hasn't,' she said tautly.

'Oh, there you two are!' Mrs Tibbs lumbered into the room. 'Just came to tell you I'm off to bed and the kids are sleeping like little logs right next door to me! So you got the place to yourselves,' she said breezily and with unmistakable implication. 'Night!'

Sarah raised her eyes heavenwards then turned back to pick up the coffee-pot.

Whereas as Cliff Wyatt said in grave accents that left her in no doubt that he was laughing inwardly, 'Well, you've got her blessing, Sarah. What more do you need?'

She moved jerkily and the pot slipped so that she poured some droplets of hot coffee on to her hand. She gasped, swallowed and bit down on any further exclamations but he was beside her in a couple of long strides. 'You little idiot,' he said roughly. 'Here, let me look!'

'No, it's nothing.'

But he possessed himself of her hand and examined the faint red mark on it. 'You're right,' he said, 'but it won't hurt to put something on it. In the meantime,

I'm going to do this, though, and don't argue with me, Sarah; it's what we both want, it's why we're both tense and impossible.'

'*I'm* not impossible——'

'Yes, you are,' he contradicted her forcefully, then his voice deepened and quietened as he added, 'Impossible to resist . . .'

She stared up into his eyes and felt her heart start to beat like a train in the moment before he lowered his head to hers.

'Why didn't you tell me?'

Sarah stirred. She was lying with her head on his shoulder, her hair splayed out across his chest, and only about five minutes before she'd climbed a pinnacle of pleasure that had left her gasping and falling and calling his name. 'Does it matter?'

'I——' He paused and slipped his hand gently through her hair. 'I ought to have known anyway.'

Sarah sat up slowly and turned to look down at him. The master bedroom was in darkness save for flickering firelight and its glow tinted her bare pale body light gold. 'I didn't want there to be any qualifications or cause for reservations; I wanted to take full responsibility for doing it . . . That's why.'

He brought his hands up to cup her breasts and said, not quite evenly, 'I was right about these. I— but Sarah, we could . . . we *should* have shared it.'

A faint smile touched her mouth. 'I don't think it could have made it any better; you didn't hurt me. Perhaps I was just a tough old virgin anyway but——'

But he drew her down into his arms again. 'There was nothing tough about you. You were—I don't know quite how to describe it.' And he frowned over her head. 'Unusually lovely.'

Sarah smiled again against the rough dark hair of his chest. 'You were breathtaking.'

He chuckled quietly. 'How do you feel now?'

'Sleepy.'

'Then let's sleep.'

She stirred. 'No. I should go back to my room.'

'There's plenty of time for that—trust me.'

'But Mrs Tibbs gets up with the birds; that's why she always goes to bed so early. So do the kids.'

'She may do. I get up even earlier. In fact I rarely sleep for more than five or six hours a night.'

'I might have known,' she said drowsily.

He pulled up the covers and took her back in his arms, and Sarah's last thought before she fell asleep was that tomorrow she would have to face the consequences of this act, but for now it was like no other feeling on earth being with Cliff Wyatt like this...

True to his word, he woke before the birds were stirring. But as her lashes fluttered up Sarah saw that he was watching her, and she saw what was in his eyes and felt the way his hands lay on her body, and a tremor rippled through her as she slipped her arms around his neck in an unmistakable gesture of acquiescence. But their second lovemaking was sweet and slow and he made her skin feel like silk and her warm, soft body feel as if it was flowering beneath his hands and his lips.

'Oh...' she said barely audibly, lying beneath him and smoothing her palms down the long, taut muscles of his back.

'I quite agree,' he murmured, holding her hard as ripples of pleasure racked them both.

A wicked little glint lit the deep blue of her naked eyes. 'It's not often we agree so—completely.'

'Ah, but I've now discovered the key to getting your agreement on things, Miss Sutherland.'

'That's a typically male kind of thing to say,' she responded gravely but with laughter in her eyes.

'I'm afraid there's a lot about me that's typically male.'

She laughed openly up at him. 'I always knew that!'

He grimaced and kissed her lightly. 'What I'm hating like hell is having to let you go so you can observe the proprieties. Do we really need——?'

Sarah moved suddenly and he rolled off her but kept her in his arms. 'Yes, we do,' she said firmly. 'Please, Cliff, let me go.'

'But there are things we need to talk about, Sarah.'

'I know. But...' she hesitated '...could I have a bit of breathing space?'

'So long as,' he said slowly and with a frown in his eyes, 'you don't use it to persuade yourself there is any cause for regret.'

She put a suddenly unsteady hand to his cheek. 'No. I doubt if I'll regret this until the day I die.'

He captured her hand and kissed her fingers and seemed about to say one thing, then change his mind. He said, 'I never did get around to putting something on your burn.'

'I'd forgotten all about it. Oh!' She raised her head as distant sounds began to make themselves heard from the kitchen.

'Don't panic,' he said wryly. 'It takes her about half an hour to stoke up the stove. And just stay there for a moment.'

She stayed and watched as he pulled on a pair of jeans and a sweater, raked a hand through his hair and rubbed the blue shadows along his jawline then gathered up her clothes and brought them to her. 'You carry these and I'll carry you.'

Her eyes widened but he wrapped her carefully in the sheet, put her glasses on then picked her up and carried her out of his bedroom and into hers where he put her into her bed and covered her up. 'Why don't you sleep in this morning, Miss Sutherland? You deserve it. I'll contrive to keep the rest of the world at bay.'

Her lips trembled into a smile. 'You're rather sweet, you know, Mr Wyatt.'

He grimaced then laughed. 'Not often, unfortunately. But——' he kissed her '—I'll see you later.'

Sarah sighed once as he left the room, then she took her glasses off, pulled the spare pillow into her arms and within minutes fell deeply and dreamlessly asleep for a couple of hours.

Which was how she came to miss Amy and Ross's triumphant arrival.

It was nine o'clock before she woke and then it took her an unusually long time to shower and dress and it didn't penetrate her consciousness that the homestead was full of talk and laughter, so deep in thought was she.

What did pierce her preoccupation briefly was how well she looked, in a rather indefinable way. As if there's been a softening and a blooming, she mused a little wryly. Is that what sex does for you? As well as making you quite unable to come to grips with the fact that you've done the unthinkable and have no idea how you're going to go on now?

She stared at her reflection in the mirror and was amazed to see herself start to blush. That was when she squared her shoulders and decided she had to face the world sooner or later.

But as she walked past the breakfast-room *en route* to the kitchen, she stopped and blinked because it was unusually full of people—Amy, looking radiant, for one. Then Sally and Ben hanging adoringly off a strange man, Cliff and, finally, Wendy Wilson. They were all tucking into a gargantuan breakfast.

It was Wendy who saw her first. 'Ah,' she said, 'our little schoolteacher. How are you, Sarah? I believe you've been making yourself absolutely indispensable,' she added in tones that were lethally insolent beneath a blatantly false and mocking little smile.

Before Sarah could answer, Cliff stood up, came towards her, smiled down at her, possessed himself of her hand and murmured, 'Come and join the mêlée. Uh...' he turned back '...Ross, this is Sarah Sutherland who's taken such good care of your kids through all sorts of traumas. Sarah, Ross and Amy have made up their—well, you can probably see all that for yourself,' he said wryly as Amy blushed and her husband, who was not particularly good-looking but had an open face and steady grey eyes, smiled at her, 'and they flew in this morning to give us the news. And,' Cliff continued, 'while I hadn't meant to spring it on everyone, I guess there's no time like the present—so the other good news is that Sarah and I are getting married.'

An absolute stunned silence greeted his words. Then Wendy started to laugh, an oddly chilling sound, and she said directly to Cliff, 'Darling, do you really think you should? Forgive me for saying so but what will that achieve? I can't help thinking it will hurt Sarah in the long run far more than it will me.'

'You're mistaken, Wendy,' he replied, quite naturally and even in friendly tones. 'Because the last thing I'll ever do is hurt Sarah.'

'How...? I don't understand. How could you?' Sarah said ten minutes later when they were closed into his study, and they were the first words she'd spoken other than mechanical thank-yous when Amy and Ross had belatedly proffered their congratulations. And she started to shake in reaction.

Cliff guided her to a chair and reached for the in-house intercom. The result was that a few minutes later, during which he'd received a telephone call with savage impatience, Mrs Tibbs arrived with a fresh pot of tea and toast.

She also directed Sarah a militant look and said, 'Heard the lot! Don't let that wild cat with the green eyes get to you!'

'Thank you, Mrs Tibbs,' Cliff said with hard authority as he put the phone down.

But she merely shrugged and took herself off.

'This is becoming a farce!' Sarah said desperately.

'No.' He poured the tea and brought it to her with some toast. 'No,' he said again as she looked up at him a little blindly. 'Don't say anything until you've had something to eat.'

'I...all right but I don't think I'm the one who should be saying things other than...how could you?' she repeated helplessly.

He sat down on the corner of the desk and simply waited until she drank some tea and ate half a slice of toast. 'Because it's what I intended to do anyway,' he said at last. 'From right after we made love for the first time last night.'

'But you can't...you can't marry me against my will, all else aside.'

'Against your will, Sarah?' he said very quietly with a narrowed, intent look that pierced her to the core.

She felt the hot colour come to her cheeks and closed her eyes briefly then said doggedly, 'I never meant it to come to this, Cliff. I did what I did last night because it seemed inevitable. It...I...for reasons best known to myself, I just wanted to do it,' she said bravely. 'But I'm not for you and, perhaps more importantly, you're not for me.'

'Why?' he said simply.

For a moment she could only look at him with hurt amazement in her eyes.

'I don't mean that,' he said roughly. 'You don't have to take her into consideration at all. Just tell me why we wouldn't—make a rather excellent team, in fact.'

Sarah tried to concentrate but she blinked several times with the effort. 'Basically I'm quite a boring person,' she said at last. 'I'm a plodder and a potterer, I'm...just not the high-flying kind of person I would associate with you.'

'What makes you think I'm such a high-flyer?' he queried with some irony. 'There's nothing exactly high-flying about what I've been doing these past weeks. I've all but worked myself to the bone,' he said with a sudden little glint of humour.

'I know,' Sarah said slowly, 'but I've always thought there are two Cliff Wyatts, the cattleman and... something rather different. Whereas there aren't two Sarah Sutherlands. After all, I've spent the last few years *proving* that to——' She stopped abruptly and went a bit pale.

'What do you mean?' he asked with a frown. 'Proving what?'

'It doesn't matter,' she said rapidly. 'Look, Cliff, not that it's going to make a difference but you can't just gloss over the subject of Wendy Wilson. To *any* prospective wife.'

He was still frowning as his gaze roamed her face and she thought, when he did speak, that there was a slightly abstracted quality to his words, as if his thoughts were elsewhere. 'What do you want to know? That she's tried to drag me to hell and back a couple of times? She has.'

He paused, saw the shock in her eyes, and suddenly focused more intently on her. 'But it's over; it's been over for years and all this... trying to blow life on to cold ashes is just a waste of time. She seized the opportunity of Amy's split with Ross to try to ingratiate herself once again—it didn't work. And, Sarah——' he raised a hand as she opened her mouth '—I'm not proud of this nor am I trying to excuse it, believe me, but there are some occasions when men will be men, unfortunately. That night on the veranda was one of them. But I *didn't* accept her other invitation—which was to sleep with her.'

'And you didn't decide to punish her this morning for the years of hell and... whatever by telling her you were going to marry me the way you did?' Sarah said very quietly. 'That's a little hard to believe, Cliff.' She stood up. 'I think we should just forget all about this before——'

'And decide we were simply ships passing in the night?' he said with gentle satire. 'Sarah——' he stood up and came over to her and put his hands about her waist '—can you honestly tell me that's what it felt like for you?'

She trembled as the memories of it came back to flood her and, as if he could read her mind, he added, 'No, it wasn't like that—because it never could be that way for you, could it? Not you... So I think you'd better tell me who you've been proving certain things to for so long, and why.'

'That doesn't really have anything to do with this, Cliff,' she said. 'You said you made this decision after the first time we made love last night. Why?'

He lifted a wry eyebrow. '*You* said something about being a boring sort of person—it certainly didn't bore me to sleep with you last night. In fact the way you did it——'

'There wasn't any special *way* I employed last night,' she objected huskily.

'I know. All the same it was a revelation.'

And as she stared up at him Sarah suddenly thought she understood. 'Because I was a virgin?' she whispered. 'Is that why...?'

His hands moved on her suddenly and she thought she saw something bleak and bitter in his eyes but it was gone before she could be sure as he said, 'Because you've got no idea how much I need you, Sarah.'

But, although he drew her into his arms then, in her heart of hearts she discovered that she believed two things—that Cliff Wyatt did need her, or thought he did, but to help him forget Wendy Wilson, and that she'd given herself away last night by surrendering her virginity to him as she had. Given him the secret she'd even tried to hide from herself, had tried to fight so hard and so unsuccessfully—that she'd fallen deeply in love with him. She believed, she realised, that he saw himself responsible for all of it.

'Cliff——'

'No, Sarah.' And he silenced her by starting to kiss her.

They were married five days later.

CHAPTER SIX

FIVE days later Sarah stood at the window of the main bedroom staring out over the darkened garden, twisting a brand-new wedding-band and a very lovely old pearl and diamond engagement ring on her left hand.

Her wedding ceremony had taken place that afternoon on the homestead veranda before a pastor who had flown in and everyone on the property had been invited. Between them Mrs Tibbs, Jean and Cindy Lawson and Amy of all people—but this was a different Amy—had provided quite a feast, and it had been touching to find that everybody was apparently absolutely delighted at this turn of events— touching but not wholly reassuring to Sarah that she was doing the right thing.

And her mind roamed back to a conversation she'd had with Amy the day after Cliff had informed her and the world at large that they were to be married . . .

'Sarah—Sarah, can I talk to you?'

Sarah was in her cottage, sorting through things, and she dusted her hands and said, 'Of course. Come in, Amy. Shall we have some tea or coffee?'

And it was helpful to make coffee while Amy made several false starts. But finally she said haplessly, 'I've been in an awful position, Sarah. Cliff is my brother and Wendy is my best friend. But you've been absolutely marvellous to my children so...' And she trailed off again.

Sarah smiled slightly and handed her her coffee. 'You don't have to explain anything, Amy. I understand.'

'Well, yes, I do and Ross agrees with me,' Amy said with more spirit. 'But I got such a shock yesterday when Cliff sprang the news on us like that and I knew Wendy...well, I probably don't have to tell you that she and Cliff go way back?' And she glanced cautiously and questioningly at Sarah.

'Yes, he told me,' Sarah said equitably.

Amy immediately looked relieved. 'They were engaged once; they just seemed like the ideal couple to start with, but...well, something happened and I don't think Cliff has ever forgiven her for it, although...but anyway,' she said hastily, 'when Ross and I——' she swallowed '—had our problem, I really needed a shoulder to cry on so I turned to Wendy. Cliff wasn't that sympathetic, you see, although I always knew he'd look after me, and while all that was going on I thought that the spark had come back for them, and I know *she* thought the same. Was I ever wrong!' She stopped helplessly and grimaced. 'About Cliff, anyway. But what I came to say was—and Ross agrees with me—that as Cliff's wife you'll have my... affection and support, Sarah.'

Sarah studied her wordlessly for a moment and wondered how two such different personalities could be brother and sister. But she said, 'Thank you, Amy, I appreciate it. Does Cliff know you're—doing this?'

'Oh, no!' Amy looked horrified. 'He told me it was none of my business and to butt out. He...I...oh, well,' she said helplessly, 'I got a bit upset about the way he bundled her off the place yesterday morning. Ross says I was wrong there but, well, you have to agree it was an awful position to be in.' And she gazed appealingly at Sarah.

'Of course,' Sarah agreed. 'And do you know, in one respect I agree with Cliff? But only this,' she said as Amy's face started to fall. 'I'm so happy for you and Ross; I like him very much and you have two super kids—I don't think you should worry about anyone else at the moment!'

'Oh, thank you, Sarah,' Amy said gratefully.

Mrs Tibbs had been much more unequivocal. 'Doing the right thing, Sarah!' she'd said at the first opportunity.

'Mrs Tibbs,' Sarah had replied, 'thank you but only weeks ago you were recommending Tim Markwell to me.'

'Forget the veterinarian—the boss will suit you much better,' Mrs Tibbs had said, quite unabashed.

Sarah had looked at her curiously and been unable to restrain herself from saying, 'Just as a matter of interest, what makes you so sure of that?'

'The man makes you come alive, that's why, Sarah, which is what it's all about even when you can find all sorts of reasons that say it's not the right bloke. Besides which, although he may not be all sweetness and light, I don't think he's a bad bloke all said and done. You could do a hell of a lot worse.' The door clicked open behind Sarah and she turned from the window to see Cliff come in but he didn't come across to her immediately. Instead, he studied her comprehensively for a long moment—the simple but beautiful Wedgwood-blue dress she wore with its long skirt—

her one good dress; her loose hair that Amy had insisted on dressing, taking two wings back from Sarah's face and pinning them behind her head with a frothy confection of white and blue ribbons that she'd made; the way she was still twisting her rings—and he said, a little drily, she thought, 'Well, Mrs Wyatt?'

'Well, Mr Wyatt,' Sarah responded, but uncertainly.

'Don't look like that, Sarah.'

'How am I looking?' she asked huskily.

At last he crossed the bedroom towards her. 'A bit like Alice in Wonderland. Bemused.'

'I would have thought I was too old to look like Alice in Wonderland, Cliff.' She tilted her head as he stopped right in front of her.

'No,' he said very quietly and put the tips of his fingers to her cheek. 'Not to me. I take it you're still cross with me for—forcing you into this marriage?'

'You didn't force me, Cliff,' she said unevenly.

'Seducing you into it, then, despite your better judgement?'

Her colour fluctuated but she said nothing.

'Isn't that why you forbade me to have any further—intercourse with you until the deed was done? Why you...' he paused '...even removed yourself to your house for the last five days?'

'That doesn't sound like being seduced into anything but no,' she said. 'I did that to observe the proprieties.'

'Well, the proprieties have now been thoroughly observed,' he said thoughtfully.

'Yes. Cliff...' She stopped and closed her eyes as he traced the outline of her mouth with one finger.

'Sarah,' he said very quietly, 'look at me.' And when her lashes fluttered up at last he went on, 'Why don't you let me show you how good a husband I can be? In other words, why don't you stop worrying about all sorts of things and—let the proof be in the pudding?' A wicked little glint lit his eyes and his lips twisted wryly. 'Not the best choice of words perhaps.'

'Only if you'll let me say this, Cliff,' she whispered. 'I've been trying to say it for days but...' She lifted one hand helplessly. 'I...slept with you, and now I've married you to some extent with things between us that I don't know about. My...' she hesitated ' ...if you like rationale to myself has been that I believed you when you said you needed me and I found I...had some needs of my own. I thought about what you said in the context of us being an excellent team and you have proved to me that a lot of things that matter to me, such as Donald Lawson and that kind of thing, mean something to you too. I also...love this place and this life.'

'And while we're on the subject,' he said, again rather drily, 'I think we should clarify your erstwhile conviction that I was too much of a high-flyer for you, Sarah.' He raised a hand as she started to object. 'In the context, my dear, that you're a very well-educated, cultured person and despite your affinity for country people you wouldn't be at all unused to or out of place in a higher society, for want of a better word.'

Her eyes widened and she said uncertainly, 'How do you know...? I mean—what do you mean?'

'It's obvious,' he said with a touch of impatience.

She relaxed a little. 'Perhaps, but what I was trying to say before you side-tracked me was that all of the reasons I married you for would count for nothing if I ever came to believe you felt yourself tied to me, and in those circumstances the least hurtful thing you could for me would be to...cut the ties.'

'So you don't really trust me but you've decided to take a punt on me anyway?' His dark eyes mocked her.

'Cliff, I'm trying to tell you it's not your fault I fell in love with you——'

'That's the best news I've had all week, Sarah.'

She bit her lip. 'I'm also trying to tell you it's not your fault I was a virgin but if you do ever decide Wendy Wilson is in your heart and your blood despite whatever it was she did to you, then I'm telling you that I came into this marriage...aware that it could be a possibility.'

'What makes you so sure of that?'

She sighed. 'I didn't say I was sure of it. On the other hand, you yourself have accused me often enough of being such a down-to-earth, common-sense sort of person——'

'I've changed my mind about that,' he said gravely.

She blinked behind her glasses. 'Why?'

'Because of the way you made love to me. There was nothing down-to-earth about it at all.'

'Cliff, we keep coming back to that,' she said helplessly. 'You've—every time I've tried to say all this you've...you've...' She stopped.

'Reminded you of it?' he suggested politely.

'*Yes*! And worse...'

'Kissed you, held you—that sort of thing?'

'Cliff...'

'What a cad,' he murmured but she could see the laughter lurking in his eyes. 'I told you I was a hard man to say no to.'

'But don't you understand that that makes me wonder if *I* am——?' She stopped abruptly.

The laughter left his eyes. 'If you're what, Sarah?'

'Nothing...nothing. Look, this is an impossible conversation—at least, you're making it so!'

'That could be because it's my wedding night,' he said idly.

She trembled and blushed.

He saw it all and continued in the same idle way, 'It could have something to do with the fact that we're really on our own at last, what with Amy, Ross and the kids on their way back to Coorilla and even Mrs Tibbs gone walkabout for our first couple of nights together, as she put it to me. "So you can do what you like—wander around starkers if you're so inclined, play hide and seek in the nuddy—different things turn different people on"...is what she also said to me.'

Sarah opened her mouth, closed it then said, 'She didn't!'

'She did—after a few glasses of champagne admittedly but it was her—er—way, I gather, of contriving to let me know you felt a bit, well, conscious of being the object of such interest and attention and possibly inhibited by it all. Not that I needed to be told that.'

Sarah frowned, all but choked and raised her hands to her face as a sudden gurgle of laughter forced its way up.

'That's better,' Cliff said barely audibly and took her into his arms.

'Oh, dear.' She laid her head on his shoulder and breathed shakily several times.

*　*　*

'This dress,' he said some time later when they were sitting side by side, hand in hand on the edge of the bed, 'did you make it, by the way?'

'No... why do you ask?'

'I thought you might have run it up for the wedding while you were insisting on living away from me.'

'No, I didn't—I doubt if I could emulate Balmain— but I hadn't ever worn it before so I thought it could be suitable.'

'Do you mean...' he looked into her eyes and his were so teasing yet warm that she felt she would die for him '...that you brought it to outback Queensland on the off-chance that you'd have the opportunity to get married in it?'

'No!' she protested. 'I actually brought a lot of my possessions to Edgeleigh—my sewing machine, my compact-disc player, books and so on—but I know what you mean about this dress; it doesn't quite fit the image of an outback schoolteacher. My... father gave it to me.'

'Correct me if I'm wrong but if it's a Balmain it probably came from Paris.'

'It did,' Sarah said briefly.

'Don't you want to tell me anything about your father, Sarah?'

'No,' she said quietly.

He didn't pursue it but said, 'Getting back to this dress, what I was actually wondering in the first place was whether you'd give me permission to take it off.'

'Considering it is all but off——' she looked down at the open front and his hand lying on her breasts beneath a oyster silk and lace bra, then up into his eyes '—I wonder you feel you need to ask permission!'

'Ah, but that's the very correct sort of guy I am, Mrs Wyatt,' he responded soberly and seriously.

'Actually, I think you're the opposite,' she said with a quiver in her voice that wasn't solely laughter as he circled first one nipple then the other with his thumb.

'So long as you don't hate me for it.'

'No...'

And finally she was free of her dress and her equally beautiful and expensive underclothes and he was still sitting on the bed but she was standing before him; he'd taken her glasses off and was running his hands down her body.

'I told you what I suspected I would find beneath your clothes, didn't I?' he murmured. 'Something delicate and shapely...I was so right.' And he nuzzled her breasts gently so that she drew a tortured breath at the exquisite torment of it and put her hands about his head as she said his name shakily.

'You're right,' he responded. 'Enough of this; it's making me slightly crazy...with desire.' And a few minutes later when he'd got rid of his clothes and they were lying together he added, 'Extremely...desirous, as you can probably tell.'

'I can,' she whispered.

'Do you think you feel the same?'

Her lips curved. 'Try me...'

But some minutes later she wasn't smiling, because once again she was falling and calling his name as pure physical rapture rocked her, and he had to hold her hard to bring her back to earth.

'Oh!' she gasped and buried her face in his shoulder. 'How can you do this to me?'

'I don't know. I mean...' he paused and stroked her hair '...you have a way of coming that's—unique.'

'I don't think it's me, it's you,' she replied with some agitation.

'Sarah—don't. Relax,' he said gently. 'It's mutual, actually.'

And gradually she quietened until finally she was able to say with some wonder in her voice, 'I didn't know I . . .' But she stopped in some frustration at not being able to find the right words.

'Well, I'll tell you something that should interest you.' He was still stroking her hair. 'Men have a fatal fascination for women who don't advertise their sensuality to the world. There's a primitive urge in us, I think, to want our women to be very private about this.'

'I'm sure I should be able to poke holes in that theory or come up with some contraindications but right at the moment I can't,' she said wryly.

He moved her away slightly so that he could look into her eyes, and said with his old, lazy amusement, 'We should have a bet.'

'A . . . what kind of a bet?'

'Are you right or am I? That kind of bet.'

'How would we prove it, though?'

'I said something earlier about the proof being in the pudding.'

Sarah looked at him narrowly but then it seemed to her as if they were straying into dangerous territory so she merely said, 'OK.'

He laughed. 'That sounds like a bit of a cop-out, Mrs Wyatt.'

'Not at all. I'm merely being cautious, Mr Wyatt. I'm not a gambler by nature.'

'It's funny you should say that, because neither am I. But I'd still like to bet I can prove it to you.'

'All right. I'll tell you when you have.'

'I'm afraid I'll have to extract a promise for that.'

'All right, I promise!' Sarah said but he only laughed at the urgency in her voice and kissed her lightly then settled her comfortably in the crook of his arm and pulled the covers over them.

He then said, 'There are some things we should discuss. Things you didn't give me the opportunity to say before you married me.'

'I . . .' But she bit her lip and amended what she'd been going to say to, 'Such as?'

'Such as whether you want to continue teaching school, whether you have the slightest interest in what you've married into, such as my ambitions in life, my philosophies on life, such as whether we'll have two children or ten—those kind of things,' he said gravely, but added on a different note, 'And why you declined even to tell me about your family, why you—married me out of hand and refused my offer to at least contact them, if nothing else.'

'Out of hand!' Sarah murmured. 'It was the other way round... However, Cliff...' she hesitated, putting her hand on his chest and twirling the rough dark hair through her fingers gently '...I don't have much family. My mother died when I was about ten and my father remarried. She, my stepmother, was much younger than he was and she only married him, I believe, for his money. She turned our lives upside-down; all she appeared to be interested in was socialising. I don't think she was faithful to him when he was alive and I know that since he died about three years ago she's taken a series of ever-younger lovers. When I took this job on Edgeleigh I didn't even tell her where

I was going I was so...upset with her.'

'So is she the one you've been proving things to, Sarah?'

She was silent for a long time. Then she said with a sigh, 'I suppose so. I grew to hate the kind of life she lived—the endless parties, the endless clothes, the endless men. I hated seeing my father become a cold, formal shell of himself—I think I grew up with the burning ambition to be as different from her as I could. Only, when this happened to me, I couldn't help wondering how different,' she said honestly.

'Sarah, if you're comparing this to——'

'I know,' she said, 'there appears to be no comparison but by the same token it's not a straightforward case of two people falling in love either.'

'Well, there's certainly been little that's been straightforward about it—that doesn't mean to say it can't be the genuine, solid-gold kind of thing. How did you feel about it several minutes ago?'

She moved against him involuntarily, and sighed. 'That's not fair.'

'You know what they say,' he replied placidly.

'About love and war?'

'Yes.'

'I'll tell you what I know——'

'Yes, do,' he teased. 'You often do it to me and I generally find it quite fascinating.'

'Then I won't—well, I really didn't think you'd sink to using tired old clichés, Cliff Wyatt, but I won't say any more.'

'That was enough and, my essential Sarah, I'm perfectly satisfied. But we still haven't worked out how you want to live your life now, Mrs Wyatt.'

Sarah realised that she was still stroking his chest at the same time as she realised that she wasn't going to get a serious conversation out of her husband of so few hours and her fingers faltered briefly at the implications of it, but then she continued curling springy bits of hair round them and said, 'Would you mind if we went on as before?'

'With certain reservations.'

'I mean, if I did go on teaching et cetera.'

'No,' he said slowly. 'If it's what you want to do but it won't always be practicable. For example, I acceded to your request for no honeymoon because there's still so much that needs to be done here but you won't be able to put me off forever, and I won't want to be leaving you behind every time I have to go away. But what would be practicable would be for us to look around for another teacher and——' he stilled the sudden tremor that ran through her '—you could still help out when you wanted to.'

That was when, Sarah later realised, the full impact of what she'd done hit her and she could only marvel that despite the trauma of the last five days, despite the sheer weight of his siege, and that was what it had been—an unrelenting assault on her physical response to him even though she'd refused to go to bed with him—something she now realised he'd even used skilfully—despite it all, she'd never done what she should have, and that was to sit down and think of how her life would have to change . . .

'Sarah?'

'Yes?' she said, but a bit shakily.

'Believe me, there'll be consolations to losing your beloved school—and you won't be losing it entirely anyway.'

'No...'

He propped himself up on one elbow and looked down at her and when he spoke again it was with no inflexion other than one of authority as he said, 'Sarah, this *will work*.'

But she could only look up at him helplessly until he swore beneath his breath and then gathered her close and just held her.

It worked for a couple of months.

'I told you this would work.'

'So you did but it's not very nice to keep saying "I told you so".'

'My dear Sarah——' Cliff paused as he was buttoning up a fresh white shirt '—your Balmain dress is becoming invaluable, incidentally.'

They were dressing for Cindy Lawson's wedding and she looked down at herself a little anxiously. 'You don't mind, do you? It's just that after all the rush to get her dress finished and help out with the bridesmaids' dresses I suddenly realised I didn't have anything appropriate to wear myself other than this.'

'Why should I mind?'

'Well, it was my wedding-dress.'

'And sort of sacred as such?'

'Well...' Sarah hesitated.

He crossed the bedroom to her. 'No, I don't mind. So long as you're always with me when you wear it, so long as I'm going to be the one to take it off you— I have to tell you, it brings back remarkable memories that I'm keen to repeat.' He put his hands around her waist and looked gravely into her naked eyes.

'That . . . goes without saying,' Sarah replied a little breathlessly and, to counter it, finished doing up his shirt buttons for him.

'There are a lot of things that go without saying,' he murmured, 'but is the doing pleasing you, Sarah?'

She looked up at last with her hands smoothing the crisp cotton. 'Yes, Cliff.'

'Is that all?'

'I'm . . . not a great one for putting these things into words.'

'Then could I expect a demonstration when this bash is over?' His hands moved down to the curve of her hips.

'I expect so.'

His lips twisted. 'Have you any idea how tantalising that is, Sarah?'

She felt the colour rising to her cheeks and bit her lip. Because, truth be told, she was still stunned after three weeks at the urgency of their lovemaking, and how, with just a look or a remark, he could draw her mind irresistibly to their bedroom and what would take place when next they were behind its closed door. But, she reminded herself, she was not totally lost to all good sense, so she said, with a swift look up at him from beneath her lashes before she then concentrated on his third button, 'If you expect me to believe you will wait around to be invited to . . . to . . .' She stopped.

'Wait around to be invited to bring you back here to bed?' he suggested.

'Yes—I don't for one minute believe it.'

He removed his hands from her hips and covered her own on his shirt-front. 'I'm undone at being so accurately assessed.'

'And I don't believe that for one minute either!'

He started to laugh then he said wryly, 'Oh, well, you may not believe this but I am undone now and, before you say another word, I think I'd better just do this.'

Which was to kiss her fairly comprehensively.

In some ways, Cindy's wedding was a strange experience for Sarah. Because, she diagnosed, it was their first official occasion together and for the first time she was acutely conscious that she was now a matron with a husband, but not just a husband—a man whom everyone present looked up to and the kind of man most women secretly dreamed about.

Is this really me? she thought once as she also detected a subtle change in everyone's attitude towards her. Not that they were any less friendly but there was a new respect, and she found herself feeling a little guilty about it and wondering, with a tinge of irony, what she'd done to earn it.

But it was a great success, Cindy's wedding, and the dress was the object of much admiration—indeed, Cindy's radiance did manage to outweigh all the pearl beads.

In fact such was the success of the wedding that as they walked down the central passageway of the homestead afterwards Sarah slipped off her shoes and murmured, 'I'm exhausted.'

'That's what the Pride of Erin does to you,' Cliff said wryly. 'You didn't tell me you were such an expert at all those old-fashioned dances. I had to fight my way through an absolute throng to get to you.'

She smiled faintly. 'I wasn't until I came to Edgeleigh.'

He stopped her with a hand on her shoulder and tilted her weary face up to him. 'I have a plan, Mrs Wyatt. Take yourself off and have a bath. Then hop into bed. I'll join you there.'

He did but he brought with him a bottle of French champagne and an artistically wrought platter of cold ham, cheese, asparagus and salad.

Sarah glanced at it in some surprise. 'Is Mrs Tibbs about?'

'Mrs Tibbs will be under a table by now. No, this is all my own work. I don't know about you but the food and champagne found at weddings in general leave a lot to be desired, I find.'

Sarah grimaced. 'They went to so much trouble.'

'I know, I'm not knocking them. But I thought a quiet, peaceful glass or two wouldn't go astray.'

'You were right,' Sarah said some time later, when she was feeling deliciously relaxed.

He removed the tray from between them and came back to bed.

'I suppose,' she said dreamily, as she slid her fingers through his hair and down his neck to his bare shoulder, 'now is the time for me to prove I'm not a . . . tantaliser.'

He slid her nightgown off her shoulder. 'It wouldn't go astray either actually. I've been in a certain amount of pain this long afternoon.'

'Oh? Why is that?' she queried innocently.

'I've had to put up with seeing a whole lot of other men dancing with you. I've had to watch you, looking so slim and lovely in your lovely dress, and count the minutes until I could get you away.'

Sarah laughed softly. 'I don't know if it's all this champagne but sometimes you do say very nice things, Cliff.'

He flicked open some buttons, drew the nightgown away from her breasts and murmured, 'I wonder why? I have a feeling it has a lot to do with these and my absolute fascination with them.'

'There are some things I find fascinating about you,' she said seriously.

'Tell me.'

'I don't think I could except to say that when you do—that——' he'd bent his head and was teasing each nipple in turn with his tongue '—I...get goose-bumps all over me.'

He lifted his head and laughed silently down at her and there was so much vitality in his eyes as well as amusement that she caught her breath. He said, 'I'll tell you what gives me goose-bumps—when you arch your body and it's like a silken, quivering bow—that really gets to me.'

'Now you're waxing lyrical,' she whispered. 'I'm sure I—don't.'

'Want to bet? Wait and see.' And his hands moved down her body, flicking open the rest of her buttons and coming to rest on the tops of her thighs.

She took a breath because she knew what would come next. Knew how, with the lightest touch, he would seek the most intimate, vulnerable part of her—and it happened. She made a husky little sound and arched her body towards him just as he'd predicted.

They had two slight disagreements over those couple of months. The first came regarding the contents of the cupboards Mrs Tibbs had shown her.

Cliff said to her one morning, 'I don't know if you're aware of it, Sarah, but there's a treasure trove of linen, crystal, silver and art work stuck away somewhere.'

'I . . . yes, I do know,' she confessed, and added, 'Mrs Tibbs showed it to me.'

He raised an eyebrow at her. 'Recently?'

'No, when I sprained my ankle.'

'Well, I haven't noticed any of it about. Why don't you get into it? A lot of it comes from my mother and she would hate to think of it all locked away.'

Sarah fingered the space on her finger where her engagement ring resided when she wore it, which wasn't often—the beautiful pearl and diamond ring had been his mother's too. And she wondered how to explain the curious reluctance she'd felt about 'getting into it' when she couldn't explain it to herself.

'I . . . tell me about your mother, Cliff. I've been meaning to ask, especially since I'm wearing her ring now.'

'Not often,' he commented with a glance at her left hand.

'That's because I'm terrified of losing it or damaging it.'

'My mother,' he said reflectively, 'was a lot like Amy. Ultra-feminine, petite but with a wonderful sense of style, a wonderful hostess, and when she wasn't being the bane of my father's life he adored her.'

'I think that's how it will be with Amy and Ross,' Sarah said wryly.

'I think you're right. Sarah,' Cliff said, and paused. They'd just finished breakfast but were still sitting at the table. 'Why don't you want to unpack those things?'

She looked away then back into his eyes. 'I don't know,' she said honestly.

'You're not still labouring under the delusion that I'm going to dump you one day and race back to Wendy?' he said harshly.

'No,' she said barely audibly. 'All right I will.' And the conversation ended as the phone rang.

She didn't see much of him for the rest of the day, nor did she unpack anything, and that evening, although he said nothing further, she felt there was a loss of ease between them but, because they were both tired, asked herself if she was imagining it. Her honest answer was that she wasn't and she was both amazed and horrified to discover how desolate she felt. And no amount of telling herself that she genuinely hadn't had the time to unpack anything helped.

She started on the cupboards the next day, which was a Saturday. But, although when Cliff came home that evening after another tiring day dipping cattle he must have noticed some of the lovely ornaments she'd unpacked, he said not a word.

Now I'm not going to start a fight over this, Sarah warned herself. After all, I've always thought privately that a lot of the quarrels married couples have are incredibly trite and silly. It's just ... well, I have to confess that I'm feeling reproachful and miserable.

Nor was it any help when, right on cue, Cliff said, 'Would you care to come and sit beside me, Sarah, and tell me what's bothering you?

They were having a pre-dinner drink in the lounge and after the barest hesitation she carried her drink over and sat beside him on the leather settee. 'Nothing.'

'Now I know damn well that's not true,' he murmured and sat back, leant his head on his hand and studied her meditatively while she sat bolt upright beside him.

Sarah moved her head in a gesture of annoyance. 'I don't see how you can know anything like that!'

'It's got something to do with the set of your chin, the particularly straight carriage of your spine plus a now in-built radar system that tells me when you're dying to give me a piece of your mind—I've had some experience of it, you see.'

She grimaced and said somewhat forlornly, 'It's never done me much good, has it?'

He started to laugh, stopped, drew in a breath and exhaled it slowly.

Sarah turned to him immediately. 'What's the matter?'

'Nothing.'

'Yes, there is!' she insisted. 'You sounded as if you were in pain.'

'Only a little. It'll pass,' he said reluctantly.

She got rid of her drink and sank to her knees in front of him. 'Cliff,' she said urgently, 'tell me!'

'It's nothing, really, Sarah. 'I—fell off the top of the cattle race this afternoon and by the feel of it bruised a few ribs. It was an extremely undignified thing to do and my pride is much more battered than I am, I can assure you.' He smiled at her ruefully.

'Let me see.'

'Sarah——'

'Cliff Wyatt, for once in your life just do as you're told!'

'Yes, ma'am.'

'No wonder you didn't notice any ornaments!' she said about ten minutes later. 'Cliff, are you sure you haven't broken any ribs? You've got the most spectacular bruising all over your back.' She rested her fingers ever so lightly on his long, powerful back that was indeed black and blue.

'No, I don't think so.'

'But how can you be sure?'

'I think I'd be in more pain. Sarah, would you do me a favour and not make too much fuss?'

She had to smile. 'All the same, lie on the bed and I'll consult Mrs Tibbs. She has a whole array of old-fashioned remedies at her command—she'll know what's best for you.'

He groaned and started to protest but Sarah marched away determinedly.

Later that night when they were in bed together, she said, 'How do you feel now?'

'Terrible.'

'Cliff...' She sat up anxiously but then she saw the wicked little glint in his eye and subsided with a militant look.

'Well, if not terrible,' he amended, 'certainly in need of some tender loving care.'

'You're a fraud.'

'I am not!' He sat up looking genuinely indignant. 'I'm just not—*that* bad.'

Her lips curved. 'All right, lie down again and I'll see what I can do.'

'That's lovely,' he said drowsily a few minutes later as she stroked him. 'I'm sorry I didn't notice the ornaments.'

'That's OK.'

'You don't sound altogether convinced.'

'I'm . . . I am. But . . . were you cross with me about it last night?'

'I . . . yes. I'm altogether over it, though.'

'So you jolly well should be,' she said, but with a smile in her voice.

'I'll remember that,' he replied meekly, which she knew was an absolute sham but as she thought of the awful bruises on his back and as she stroked away gently her heart, curiously, she discovered, was full of love.

Their next disagreement was the one that led indirectly to much more serious consequences—consequences that she never in her wildest dreams expected.

CHAPTER SEVEN

IT WAS strange how from the day that she started to unpack those cupboards whatever had been holding her back dried up and she suddenly found herself assuming a new role.

Up until then, she realised, although she'd married Cliff, although she'd gloried in sharing his bed, she'd continued her life very much as it had been before. But now she found the homestead claiming her as it had threatened to do once before, but the problem was that she also found she just didn't have enough hours in the day for all she wanted to do and she began to feel more and more tired.

So it came as no surprise really when Cliff said abruptly to her one night, 'I've advertised for another teacher, Sarah.'

All the same, she caught her breath and said a little dazedly, 'You could have discussed it with me first.'

'But there are things we don't ever discuss, aren't there?'

'I don't know what you mean ...'

'Well, we make no plans, you know no more than you ever did about Wyatt Holdings, what other properties are involved or even if I'm winning the battle here on Edgeleigh.'

For a moment she looked stricken then she said uncertainly, 'I'm sure you are. Everyone keeps telling me how ... wonderful you are.'

He breathed exasperatedly. 'That's got nothing to do with drought, flood and beef cattle prices. And these things,' he added deliberately, 'are your problem now as much as mine. In other words, your horizons have broadened a bit beyond twelve kids in a school, Sarah.'

Her eyes widened and her face paled slightly. 'I'm sorry,' she said. 'I ... you're right; I don't know why but I ... I've been remiss.'

His mouth set in a hard line then he shrugged. 'No, you haven't actually. You're the perfect wife in most respects for this kind of life. But I had hoped that by now you would see it as—well, a wider field,' he said with irony.

She started to tremble inwardly. 'How ... how can I start?'

'By letting me engage another teacher and not getting upset about it, by letting me take you away for a holiday or a delayed honeymoon and showing you what you've married into. By having the time just to be a wife.'

She put her hands together. 'Yes. If you want to; but could I just ... help you to choose this new teacher?'

For a moment she held her breath as tough, hard lines appeared beside his mouth but slowly they relaxed and a flicker of amusement came to his dark eyes as he drawled, 'Maybe I was more right about you than I thought, Sarah.'

She didn't pretend to be at a loss. 'That I'm a school-marm born and bred? Maybe—I'm sorry.'

He narrowed his eyes and for a moment she thought she glimpsed an expression of extreme frustration in them but it was gone before she could be sure. Then to her relief he put out his hand slowly and said quietly, 'Don't look like that—come here.' And when she came he took her in his arms and after a while the awful desolate feeling she'd begun to experience receded.

They chose a young man with a beard and a limp due to one leg being a bit shorter than the other, and, as one zealot to another, Sarah could tell he was as passionate about teaching as she was and had an affinity with children of all ages. He'd also been born on a cattle station and would start after the September holidays, now almost upon them.

'Satisfied, Sarah?' Cliff said.

'Yes, I really am. Thank you—for understanding.'

He looked at her wryly. 'Then you'd better pack your bags.'

'Where will we go?'

'Coorilla for a few days; the rest is to be a surprise.'

Sarah chewed her lip. 'I don't have an awful lot to wear.'

'So I've noticed.'

She hesitated and wondered if that was something else he held against her. 'Do you mind that, Cliff?' she said directly.

'Mind what?' He raised an eyebrow at her.

'That I don't bother much about clothes and make-up and so on.'

He looked at her consideringly and she held her breath. 'On the contrary,' he said at last. 'I find it a refreshing change. And that surely must put me up a step in your estimation, Sarah,' he said with a faint flicker of a smile.

'I don't—I don't quite follow.'

'Well, I'll explain. It was obviously your soul that got me in and not any extraneous gilding of the lily.'

'Is that so?' she said sweetly. 'So it wouldn't have mattered if I'd had buck teeth, pimples and weighed fifteen stone? I don't know why but that rather amazes me.'

'Ah, well, perhaps I should also tell you that you often remind me of a lily—pure, fresh and lovely.' And his dark, wicked gaze drifted slowly down her body.

Sarah laughed and blushed at the same time as she said, 'Well, now you have gone a step up in my estimation, Mr Wyatt. But by the same token I might need some more clothes—I hope that doesn't ruin my image in your eyes?'

'Not at all. I'll be delighted to help you choose them in fact.'

A sudden thought struck Sarah. 'Would you mind if I paid for them?'

'Yes, I would!'

'I mean—and don't get angry,' she said as she saw his eyes, 'that I've had nothing to spend my wages on for a long time so I could spend it on a belated trousseau—that's what brides do.'

'Sarah, if you say one more word along those lines, I'll not only get angry but I'll make love to you as you've never been made love to before!'

'Now I've offended you.' She pulled a wry face. 'It was just a thought. Do you mean the kind of love that will make me limp and breathless and not sure where I am or what day it is?'

'Exactly.'

'But you do that all the time,' she said innocently.

'You——' He broke off and the tension drained out of him and he started to laugh. 'You're becoming a minx, my dear,' he said, and he pulled her into his arms.

'I just thought I should show you there's more to me than meets the eye,' she murmured as she raised her mouth for his kiss.

'If you think I'm not getting to know *that* more and more,' he replied, 'think again.' And he would have kissed her had not an unmistakable, trumpet-like clearing of someone's throat taken place behind them.

Cliff swore beneath his breath. '*Yes*, Mrs Tibbs?'

'Now you don't need to feel embarrassed on my account, Cliff,' Mrs Tibbs replied genially. 'It'd worry me a hell of a lot if I didn't stumble on you two doing this sometimes.'

'Well, I'm so glad I'm contributing to your peace of mind, Mrs Tibbs. Is there something you wanted to say to me or are you just passing through?'

'Billy Pascoe's mum's on the line. She needs Sarah. He's gone and painted himself from head to toe with some paint he brought home from school and it won't come off. She's scrubbed him till he's about to bleed, apparently.'

'That kid needs a——' Cliff said ominously, and stopped.

'I think you might be right,' Sarah said. 'He needs a man teacher.'

She felt the jolt of laughter that went through Cliff but he said, 'I was going to say he needs a good hiding.'

'I suspect that's the only kind of attention he gets from his father, unfortunately. I'd better go——'

'Just a minute—has *she* gone?'

Sarah peeped round him. 'Yes.'

'Well, then, there's some unfinished business here to be attended to.' And he proceeded to kiss her thoroughly. When he'd finished, he said, trailing his fingers down the line of her jaw, 'Billy Pascoe's all yours now.'

They flew away from Edgeleigh in the helicopter and took Donald Lawson with them. And Amy and Ross, Ben and Sally were waiting excitedly to greet them when they landed.

Coorilla was indeed a showplace, Sarah discovered. It was a graceful two-storeyed house set in much gentler, greener countryside than Edgeleigh and it occurred to Sarah to wonder why Cliff had arranged things thus—virtually banishing himself to the wilderness and handing this lovely place over to Amy and Ross. But for the first couple of days Amy had so many activities planned for them that she hardly had time to draw breath. Then things settled down and Cliff and Ross began a detailed inspection of the property—which was how Sarah came to find herself one damp morning being regaled with the family photo albums.

She thought later that it genuinely hadn't occurred to Amy how many photos of Wendy Wilson there were in the albums and she thought this because, after stumbling across the first few, Amy grew red-faced and started to rifle through the pages awkwardly. She also thought with some exasperation that her sister-in-law really was a bit of a twit but at the time she said nothing and tried to endure the whole embarrassing business with an outward appearance of serenity.

But two of those photos seemed to imprint themselves on her brain—Cliff and Wendy's engagement photo, taken in the main drawing-room right here at Coorilla with Wendy looking straight at the camera and Cliff looking down at her, and one of Wendy in a chic uniform. And when the last album was closed she said, 'So—she's an air hostess?'

Amy looked pathetically grateful for something—probably my normal tones, Sarah thought—and she said, not without some pride, 'She's more than that now, she's a senior stewardess; it's a really top job. But I think it was one of the reasons she and Cliff broke up. She used to say she couldn't imagine herself stuck at Coorilla for the rest of her life.'

'But they got engaged despite that?'

Amy hesitated. 'She only started to say it *after* they got engaged. I think she thought she could win Cliff round to the kind of marriage where she did her own thing while she felt like it. I have to say,' Amy proceeded to say, although unhappily, 'there was always... I don't know but it was always a sort of love-hate relationship. Wendy, I see now, didn't really want to be dominated by any man. *Then*, that is—I think she's changed her thinking now. But, of course, after what she did you can't really blame Cliff for never forgiving her.'

'Did?' was all Sarah had to say for Amy to continue to unburden herself.

'Have a blazing public affair with a much older man the minute Cliff broke off the engagement. But not only that...' Amy at last realised that she might have let her indiscreet tongue run away with her and sought to regroup ' . . . she left it too late, didn't she? Because he found you, Sarah, and he's looking so . . . relaxed, I *know* it must be working.'

That night in bed, Sarah found it hard to get to sleep because she couldn't rid her mind of several things.

'Sarah?'

She moved closer to Cliff and laid her cheek on his back. 'Sorry, I just can't get to sleep. When are we leaving?'

He reached behind and stroked her thigh. 'Tomorrow if you like. I too am suffering from a surfeit of Coorilla, if that's what you're trying to say, although it's good to see Amy settled down again.'

'I'd like that,' she said, and presently fell asleep at last.

He flew her to Brisbane, hired a car and drove down the coast to Surfer's Paradise where they booked into the Sheraton Mirage, a magnificent resort hotel that looked on to the golden beach and the rolling surf of the South Pacific, and had the Marina Mirage shopping complex across the road.

Sarah's first purchase in the glamorous shopping complex was a swimsuit. Then Cliff took matters in hand and caused a flutter in all the boutiques they visited and when they got back to their room over-looking the ocean she laid the purchases out on the bed and all of them were exquisite and very expensive.

'Thank you,' she said with her mouth curving into a smile, 'but this is really gilding the lily.'

He regarded her thoughtfully for a long moment. 'It's been my pleasure,' he said at last, 'but something tells me my lily is a little troubled. You surely don't

resent my buying you clothes, Sarah? Or perceive that
it's going to turn you into a limited edition of your
stepmother?'

'No,' she said and, making a sudden resolution, she
crossed the room to him, put her arms around his
waist and laid her head on his chest. 'This truly
grateful wife has really realised that she was trying to
do more than she should, and is now suffering
from ... reaction and over-tiredness.' Which is also
true, she thought. I don't know why but I *don't* feel
quite myself ...

'Now that is something I can deal with,' he said
quietly and touched her hair lingeringly.

For the next few days they lay on the beach a lot,
walked a little, swam, ate and slept a lot. Cliff's olive
skin tanned easily and even Sarah's much paler com-
plexion took on a golden glow.

And on their fourth evening when she put on one
of her new outfits—a filmy trouser suit in a slate-blue
with a tucked bodice, no sleeves and cross-over
straps—he said to her, 'You look positively exotic,
Mrs Wyatt.' And he tucked a creamy camellia from
a vase of flowers into her hair.

Sarah studied her reflection and agreed that she did
look different. And she started to say something about
another reason why she might look different, one that
had only just occurred to her, but said instead, 'You
look absolutely splendid.' He was standing behind her
and in his long-sleeved white shirt and navy trousers
he was incredibly good-looking. 'You know,' she
added, 'maybe I should consider contact lenses.'

He put his fingers on the rounded tips of her
shoulders and she shivered at the feel of it. 'I don't

mind your glasses, Sarah.' He pulled her back against him and she revelled in the feel of his lean, hard body against her own. 'Feeling...better now?' he said very quietly.

'I'm feeling wonderful,' she replied softly.

'Good.'

But it was that same evening that everything was shattered for her.

As they crossed the foyer hand in hand towards the restaurant Sarah noticed a laughing group of airline personnel at the main doors, waiting, apparently, for their transport. There was nothing to particularly identify Wendy Wilson—she had her back to them, they were separated by the width of the foyer and if she hadn't now known the other girl was a stewardess Sarah might not have recognised her at all with her black hair tucked away beneath her hat, standing amid three other chic, tall girls. But even as her senses suddenly attuned to the uniform, Cliff tensed perceptibly beside her and his grip on her hand was briefly crushing.

She made an inarticulate sound and looked up at him to see him staring across the foyer before he looked down at her and murmured, 'Sorry—here we are.' And he gestured for her to enter the restaurant ahead of him.

'Our dinner wasn't exactly a success—want to tell me why?'

Sarah turned from the window where she'd been watching the play of white moonlight on a choppy, gunmetal sea. 'Just tired, I guess. Perhaps you were too—you didn't have a lot to say,' she added, not looking at him, then shrugged. 'Not that it matters; I'm going to bed.'

'No, Sarah,' he said in a hard voice. 'Let's have it out in plain English——'

'Plain English?' she cried, and stumbled over to the bed to sit down agitatedly. 'All right, are you going to react like that every time you see her—it was her, wasn't it, Cliff?'

He was standing across the room with his hands shoved irritably into his pockets but he came to sit beside her, catching her wrists as she immediately tried to get up. 'Sarah, calm down,' he ordered, then sighed. 'Yes, it was her, but you could be misinterpreting my reaction.'

'Cliff—Cliff——' she swallowed '—just answer these questions. Why did you give up Coorilla to come and live all the way out at Edgeleigh?'

'You should have no difficulty in understanding that,' he said shortly. 'Amy's as much entitled to it as I am and I knew she could be happy there; Ross is as good at running it as I am but two of us on the place wouldn't have worked in the long run.'

'Or were the memories just too painful to live with?' Sarah suggested very quietly. 'The memories of your engagement party for example?'

'What the hell do you know about that?'

'I saw some photos——'

'Bloody Amy, I suppose——' he said savagely, and stopped abruptly.

'You mustn't blame her; there was no malice, just—just——'

'Just Amy being her usual stupid self,' he ground out.

'They are best friends. But you haven't told me if I'm right, Cliff.'

He swore then stood up. 'All right,' he said harshly, with his back to her, 'I can't stand the place any more and I wanted to get as far away as I could. But not——' he swung round '—because of any *happy* memories, nor, for that matter, any bittersweet memories, but memories I *hate*. Memories of what an incredible fool I was, how I let myself get taken for an all-time ride by the best . . . *bitch* in the business. How I wasted years of my life on a woman who's not worth tuppence but can use her body and those green eyes like a . . . siren.'

'Cliff,' Sarah whispered.

'Then I met you,' he said. 'So much the opposite, so far removed——' he raised his hand in a gesture that was suddenly incredibly weary '—from all that kind of thing. And I thought, Why not? This is sanity and peace and I desperately need some peace, some order, some companionship and *none* of the trappings of the kind of grand passion that sucks you in and down into a vortex of—unreason.'

Some little thing wilted in Sarah's heart and died and she put her hand to her heart involuntarily as if she could feel its passing.

He stared down at her, noting the gesture, his own face now pale and scoured with lines of tension, and his voice was laden with it as he said, 'None of which means to say I don't love you, Sarah.'

'In a way? I know,' she heard herself answering as if from a great distance. 'I also can't help believing— and I don't mean to be honest in a righteous, thoroughly irritating way—but I can't help believing, Cliff, that in your heart of hearts there had to be a certain fitting sort of irony about marrying me the way you did and when you did. I just don't know...' she paused then went on barely audibly '...if I can live with it any more.'

'Well, I'm afraid you're going to have to. You told me once that you had your own rationale for doing this——'

'I know, I know,' she whispered. 'It's my fault as much as... I shouldn't have done it——'

'Sarah,' he overrode her in that cool, authoritative voice that went through her heart like a knife, 'it's done and there's no turning back now, nor should I have to tell you why. Because in about eight months from now, I imagine, to put it as Mrs Tibbs might, we'll have the patter of little feet to join us to each other forever.'

She gasped and paled. 'You...know?' And her eyes were huge and stunned behind her glasses as she stared at him.

'I can count,' he said grimly. 'Nor could we have been closer these past few months. And——' he stopped, the pressure of his fingers relaxing suddenly on her wrists and his voice changing '—I've seen you lately, these past two weeks, be different—dreamy and sleepy sometimes, *starving* sometimes, even looking a little nauseous. All of which adds up to one thing.'

'Why didn't you say something?'

'I only really put it all together a day or so ago.'

'So did I,' she confessed. 'I thought I must have got my dates mixed up at first. But Cliff——'

'No, Sarah. I'm sorry if...' he paused '...I've disappointed you, I'm sorry I'm...perhaps a rather brutalised sort of person now, but one thing I can tell you is this—your welfare and that of *our* child means more to me than anything else. It also means I'll never let you go—if that's what you had in mind this evening.'

What she would have said and done then she was destined never to know, because the phone beside the bed buzzed discreetly and he swore and picked it up. And she had little difficulty in working out that the call was from Edgeleigh, and urgent.

'What?' she said anxiously as soon as he put the phone down.

'It's raining.'

'Well, that's great news—isn't it?' she said uncertainly.

'If you consider losing half the herd good news,' he answered abruptly. 'The place is all but flooded.'

'But I thought it never flooded! I mean, I always thought drought was the problem out there.'

'It is, nine times out of ten. But once every pancake day it goes the other way. This is it.' He picked up the phone again. 'Will you be all right to leave tonight?'

'I . . . yes . . . but is it really that serious, Cliff?'

'Believe it, Sarah.'

It was a tense, long, long night but as they flew over Edgeleigh in a gloomy grey dawn Sarah believed him. 'It's like a lake,' she said incredulously.

'I know, and all the best feed is under water. At least the homestead et cetera are still clear.' He turned to her abruptly, his hands steady on the controls but his expression frustrated. 'I shouldn't have brought you back and I certainly shouldn't have put you through this kind of a night.'

'I'm fine. Just tired,' she answered steadily. 'And I can always be flown off again if there's ... any problem.'

'Do you *feel*——?'

'No, Cliff. I only said that so you won't worry about me as well as all this.' She waved a hand at the soggy view beyond the perspex dome of the helicopter.

'Well, we'll get the Flying Doctor in anyway just to check you out.'

'Cliff!' she protested.

But he said, 'Why not? In normal circumstances isn't that what pregnant women do? Start going to a doctor?'

'I suppose so ... I hadn't really thought about it.'

'Then, Mrs Wyatt, it's about time you did.'

It's about time you thought about a lot of things, Mrs Wyatt, Sarah repeated to herself in her mind that afternoon when she was rebelliously lying on their bed, supposedly taking a nap at both Cliff's and Mrs Tibbs' direction.

Cliff had actually stunned her by imparting the news of the baby to Mrs Tibbs as soon as they arrived at the homestead, thereby causing genuine joy to light up Mrs Tibbs' face and causing her to say, 'Oh, you've done well, Cliff! A little bundle of joy of her own is just what she needs to take her mind off everybody else's kids!'

And then he'd had the gall to swing round to Sarah, regard her outraged expression with a wicked little glint in his eye, and say innocently, 'I hadn't looked at it that way, but she might be right.'

'You ...' But Sarah had been genuinely lost for words.

And I'm still lost for them, she mused as she listened to the rain on the roof. I've gone from high drama to comedy in the space of a day, not that this flood is going to be funny, but . . .

I've gone from having Cliff admit that he needed sanity and companionship, not a grand passion, I've gone from thinking I couldn't stand to live with it to being back here and, I suspect, trying to go on as before . . .

'But what do you do?' she whispered aloud. 'After all, you took no precautions against this happening, you *did* go into this marriage prepared, if it was possible, to make it work, and you only made one stipulation, if you could call it that—did he breach that stipulation last night?'

Oh, come now, Sarah, she answered herself silently, didn't you always know? That you could engage his companionship, his care, but it was his heart and soul you were always worried about. Isn't it strange that you allowed yourself to be married for all the things you told him you'd rather die than . . . be married for?

And despite her rebellious mood she fell asleep not long afterwards but with tears on her lashes.

CHAPTER EIGHT

IT WAS two weeks before the floor waters began to subside, two desperate weeks during which everyone involved strained every nerve to save the far-flung herd.

It was heartbreaking to see the cattle standing knee-deep in water with no feed or bunched up on every available patch of higher ground that had escaped the creeping flood. It also gave Sarah two new insights—into the ever-present threat of natural disaster that accompanied rural life, and into the size and power of Wyatt Holdings. Because it was that that saved the day for Edgeleigh; it was being able to call on Ross and have bulk feed shipped from Coorilla to be hand-distributed to the cattle where possible and it was the manpower from three other properties in the empire that enabled a lot of cattle to be trucked off Edgeleigh until conditions returned to normal. But it was a huge operation and of course not only Edgeleigh was affected but neighbouring properties, and it amazed her how everyone bucked in and helped out where they could.

It was also she who slipped into the role of co-ordinator, mainly because Cliff refused point-blank to allow her to do anything else—provoking a rather tense little scene between them at first . . .

'Cliff, I'm not *ill*. This is a perfectly normal process and I'm perfectly normal—as the Flying Doctor *told* you!'

'I don't care what he told me—there are enough able-bodied, willing women on the place who are not pregnant and who can help out, deal with extra chores and cope with feeding everyone who comes and goes. You just stay put, Sarah, I'm warning you!'

She stared up at him in his mud-spattered khakis, at the lines of weariness beside his mouth, the grazed knuckles of one hand, the implacable look in his dark eyes. 'But it's not fair,' she said frustratedly. 'How do you think I feel sitting here twiddling my thumbs when you're so tired you——?'

'I'll be fine,' he said tersely. 'Just do as you're told.' And he turned away.

'Yes, Sarah, you do as you're told,' Mrs Tibbs repeated as soon as Cliff left the house.

Sarah opened her mouth, closed it, bit her tongue and stalked out of the kitchen.

It was Jim Lawson who put her out of her misery. He rang a bit later to ask if she would mind handling his CB radio and mobile phone for the afternoon. 'We've got a real crisis on the western boundary and I feel I should be there instead of sitting here taking calls, but someone's got to monitor things——'

'Jim, I'd be delighted to. Just bring them up to me,' Sarah said eagerly.

He did although he said, 'Hope Cliff doesn't mind; we decided one of us should co-ordinate.'

'I'll square it with Cliff,' Sarah told him. 'Just leave it to me, Jim. What's the crisis?'

'A big bunch of calves bogged in the mud.'

She winced then urged him on his way and set herself up in Cliff's study where she found maps of the property which she set out carefully, along with Jim's notes—and began to feel better.

She didn't see Cliff that night although she spoke to him on the radio a couple of times but late the next afternoon he came home for a few hours, and his lips twitched as he walked in on her in the study.

She switched off the mobile phone and said, 'If you say a word, Cliff Wyatt...!'

'Well, I was only going to say you've done well, Sarah, but if you'd rather I didn't...' He shrugged.

She stood up and eyed him militantly.

'Perhaps you're right,' he murmured. 'There are better ways than words, after all. Is that what you meant?' He took her in his arms and looked down at her gravely.

'Cliff...' She breathed a little erratically, mainly, she thought, because it was the first time it had happened since the night he'd seen Wendy Wilson, and at the back of her mind she'd wondered how she would feel—only nothing's changed there, she realised starkly.

'Sorry,' he murmured and kissed her hair lightly, 'I'm a wreck; I shouldn't be doing this until I've cleaned up.'

'No, it's not that——' She broke off abruptly then started to blush.

'What is it, then?'

'Nothing,' she said hastily. 'So you don't mind me doing this? All I have to do is sit in a chair!'

'Not only don't I mind but I'm very grateful. It frees Jim up.'

She fingered his sleeve and said in an oddly husky voice, 'You don't have to be *grateful*. I'm...part of this now, aren't I?'

He stared down into her eyes with his own narrowed and curiously probing and she thought, with her heart suddenly in her mouth, Oh, God, what have I told him? That I've decided to go on as before? I didn't even really know it myself or pretended I didn't... 'Yes, Sarah,' he said quietly, breaking into her thoughts, 'and a very special part—don't forget that.'

'Cliff...'

But he laughed down at her. 'I know what you're going to say—I need a shower. I'm off. I'm also going to try to catch some sleep. Can you wake me at seven-thirty?'

'Cliff—that's only about three hours!'

'I told you I don't need a lot of sleep.'

'Well——'

'Please, miss.'

'Oh, all right but——'

'Thank you, miss. May I go now, miss?'

She'd more or less decided not to wake him when she'd seen how deeply and peacefully he was sleeping but just before seven-thirty she got a call to say that a road train coming to pick up cattle, which they thought had been delayed until the morning, was about to arrive, so she did, reluctantly.

He rolled over as she bent over the bed and touched him gently on his bare shoulder. He mumbled something drowsily and then pulled her down beside him and started to kiss her.

'Cliff—Cliff,' she said a few moments later, a little breathlessly and not sure if he was properly awake, 'this is very nice but you asked me to wake you, not——' She broke off as he buried his head against her breasts.

'Not tantalise me as you have a habit of doing?'

'I do not!'

'Oh, yes, you do.'

She touched his hair and felt her nipples tingle so she tried again. 'Cliff—are you awake?'

He drew his head back and looked up at her with so much amusement dancing in his eyes although he said reproachfully, 'Of course I'm awake. I'd be mad to do this in my sleep—especially when we haven't done it for—I've lost count of how many days!'

'Well,' she temporised, 'I'm not sure if this is the right time either, unfortunately.'

'Oh—why is that?' And for a moment he tilted his head at her in his old, arrogant manner.

She told him and he cursed fluently but he also released her, threw the covers off and got up as he said wryly, 'You're right—unfortunately. The mob they've come to pick up is getting pretty weak. The sooner they go the better.'

She sat back and watched him pull on the clean clothes she'd laid out, and wondered when the sight of his magnificent body would stop doing strange things to her heart and her breathing.

'What's wrong, Sarah?'

She moved a bit abruptly. 'Nothing. How long is this going to last?' she asked sombrely.

He shrugged his broad shoulders. 'I think it might have peaked but although it's stopped raining it could take a while to go down—I don't know, Sarah. A long while until we get back to normal but I suppose the bright side is we'll have a really good season next season. Finding it tough?'

'No—yes.' She made a futile little gesture. 'I mean, *I'm* having it easier than anyone... I was thinking of you.'

'Well, I'm as tough as they come,' he replied cheerfully, 'so don't worry about me. How is the heir apparent taking it all, do you think?'

Her lips parted. 'The...oh! Well, apart from making me lose my breakfast with monotonous regularity there's not much that's...apparent about this heir as yet.'

He grinned. 'Well said. I always knew you were good with words, as befits any born and bred schoolteacher. But I'm told that doesn't last long—the loss of breakfast syndrome.'

Sarah chuckled. 'Now who told you that?'

'Mrs Tibbs. I have it on her good authority that you will settle down and start to—er—bloom shortly.'

Sarah grimaced. 'That's what she keeps telling me. I'm not so sure that I'm looking forward to the "blooming" process, however. I really wish I were *tall*, now I come to think of it. I've got the feeling I'm going to look like a tub on feet.'

He was brushing his hair and he came to sit down beside her. 'So long as you're not anti the process altogether.'

She looked at him enquiringly.

'Of starting a family,' he said soberly, looking down at the brush in his hands. 'It was not something we ever got around to discussing.' He looked up into her eyes.

She coloured slightly then said honestly, 'Do you know, Cliff, so much has happened since...this happened——' she put her hand on her stomach involuntarily '—that I haven't really been able to think about it a lot?'

'Fair enough,' he murmured. 'But I'd like to know if you're—hating the idea of it. If that's why you can't think about it.'

'No,' she said slowly. 'I . . . I . . . just don't think the idea that I'll be a mother shortly has sunk in yet. Perhaps . . . once I start to bloom, it will all fall into place.'

He glanced at her penetratingly then he said something that surprised her. 'Why don't you have your erstwhile school up for tea tomorrow afternoon? I'm sure you'd love it, I'm sure they'd love it and I'm sure Mrs Tibbs can provide the tea.'

Sarah sat up eagerly. 'Can I do that?'

He stood up and watched her face enigmatically for a moment before he murmured, 'Go to it, Mrs Wyatt. Just don't overdo it.'

It wasn't until some time later that she was to re-alise how cleverly Cliff was contriving to bind her to Edgeleigh, almost as if he'd foreseen the one thing that would drive her away . . .

But the weeks passed and the flood receded, leaving the land to recuperate, and slowly things did get back to normal—their marriage included although Cliff was away a lot. And it was on one of these occasions, when she was about three months pregnant, that she woke up feeling distinctly strange, and a few hours later, before either the Flying Doctor arrived or Cliff could be contacted, she suffered a miscarriage.

In fact she didn't see Cliff until she'd been flown to the nearest base hospital. And it was a white, haggard, dazed and weary face she turned to the door as he strode in to her private room.

'Sarah—for God's sake, I'm sorry.'

'So am I,' she whispered out of a dry throat, 'but it wasn't your fault.' And she buried her face against his shoulder and wept hot, miserable, guilty tears.

'I mean I'm sorry I wasn't there—that you had to go through all that on your own.'

'Perhaps I deserved it,' she wept.

He held her away and frowned down at her. 'What the hell do you mean? What were you doing?'

'Nothing! Nothing...but that was it, you see.'

'No, I don't—hang on, don't cry like that.'

She took several deep, shaky breaths and finally the way he was stroking her hair got through to her and she felt herself calming down.

'Now,' he said at last, 'tell me what you meant.'

But as she lay against his chest she knew she couldn't disclose the truth to anyone, let alone him, knew she could never tell him that until she'd started to lose his baby she'd found it almost impossible to believe she was going to be a mother, that it was as if it were happening to someone else, not to Sarah Sutherland, the one person who should never have allowed herself to be rushed off her feet into a marriage she'd had so many doubts about and then, before she'd barely had time to turn around, let herself fall pregnant. But once the painful process had begun and she'd had no answer for the powerful forces of her body she'd felt her heart starting to break for what she was losing as the realisation had suddenly and finally hit her—their child. And that it had taken this to make her think of it as such, at last.

'Sarah?'

'Oh, Cliff, I don't know,' she said hoarsely. 'I don't think I'm making any sense.'

She felt him relax slightly although the rhythmic movement of his hand on her hair didn't stop. 'That's only natural,' he said quietly. 'But the doctor's told me that as far as they can tell at this stage it was simply one of those pregnancies destined not to come to term. In other words, it's something that just happens sometimes and you could well go on to have a cricket team of babies.'

She sniffed and tried to smile as he held her away. 'Well, that's good news.' But her voice lacked conviction and although he frowned again he didn't pursue it.

She stayed in hospital for a week but she was still pale and listless when she got back to Edgeleigh, still plagued by a terrible feeling of guilt that she'd wished a child out of existence by refusing to think about it even though she told herself again and again that it wasn't sensible or rational to think that.

She also refused categorically when Cliff suggested they spend a few days on the coast, just relaxing before going home. Mainly because she was suddenly afraid to be alone with him, she realised, but also because 'Operation Noah's Ark' was going into reverse. Plenty of summer sun had wrought a miracle on Edgeleigh and the cattle were coming back so he needed to be there, and Christmas was on the way and Amy, Ross and the children were to spend it with them—all of which she one day detailed to Cliff—except her fear of being alone with him.

She held her breath as his dark gaze roamed her face critically for a long moment but beyond that he made no comment.

She also heard herself say, 'And the doctor's told me we should...we shouldn't...that is to say...' She stopped awkwardly.

'Say it, Sarah,' he commanded quietly.

She studied her hands. 'We shouldn't sleep together for a few weeks.'

'I know. He told me that too.'

It was something in his tone that made her glance up and say, 'Do you mind?' then bite her lip.

'Why should I mind?'

'Well...' She hesitated.

But he said drily, 'Of course I don't mind while you're going through a healing process; I'm neither insatiable nor a monster.'

'I didn't mean that but you did sound—I thought you sounded a bit strange,' she persevered, mainly in self-defence when she should had just shut up.

'Sarah...' He paused and seemed to change his mind. 'Forget about that. Let's just concentrate on getting you well and *happy* again.' And he covered her hand with his own and smiled at her suddenly, taking her breath away as it often did when it was unexpected. He also said lightly, 'You've still got me, you know.' And she hoped he didn't realise how those words struck at her heart.

'Sarah, only three weeks ago you had a miscarriage! Will you *sit down* and *stop* overdoing things?' Mrs Tibbs said irately. 'For one thing, I've prepared Christmas tucker and the like for fifty people in my time, let alone six, and, for another, it's *me* Cliff's going to get wild with when he comes home tonight and sees you looking all tired and washed out.' Cliff had had to go away on business for the first time since she'd got home from hospital, a night in Brisbane and a night on Coorilla, he'd told her.

'But it helps to keep busy,' Sarah replied, unwisely as it turned out.

'Helps *what*?' Mrs Tibbs tossed her dishcloth away and stood in front of her, arms akimbo. 'Now I know it's natural to pine a bit, but when they've told you they can see no reason for it to happen again you're mad if you don't put it all behind you! You've got a wonderful husband and I just hope you aren't stupid enough still to be worried about that she-cat with the green eyes. He's *done* with her. What more do you expect him to do to prove it?'

'I don't . . . it's not that.'

'Then stop fiddling and fretting and start eating properly—I would never have expected *you* to be so simple-minded, Sarah Sutherland.'

She wasn't sure whether it was the Sutherland bit or the reference to Wendy or the reference to Cliff that did it but all of a sudden Sarah felt her hackles rise and she said, 'Mrs Tibbs, I'm grateful for your concern but I'd be a lot more grateful if you'd mind your own business!'

But it didn't have quite the desired effect because Mrs Tibbs said complacently, 'Now that's more like it—suits you much better, Sarah, than getting round like a wet weekend who can't sit still.'

Sarah ground her teeth and stalked away.

But when Cliff did come home it swiftly became evident that he was not in a good mood, although not, as it turned out, over Sarah's looking tired and washed out. In fact she never actually discovered what had first caused his black mood but she certainly heard it first hand...

She first of all heard the helicopter arriving and if she hadn't been in the middle of making a cake, which Mrs Tibbs had only allowed her to do after she'd had an afternoon rest, she would have gone down to meet him. But by the time she'd got it into the oven and rinsed her hands he'd arrived at the homestead but gone straight into his study from where he'd proceeded to set the place by its ears.

'Told you,' Mrs Tibbs said as they both stood listening with some awe to what he was saying on the phone to Jim Lawson.

'He hasn't even set eyes on me,' Sarah protested.

'Well, something's got him worked up good and proper. I'm only glad I'm not Jim.'

'But it's hardly fair; everyone worked so hard during the flood——'

'Sarah, Sarah, those fences he's carrying on about have been missing since the flood and it's vital they get put up again.'

'But that's still not Jim's fault—I was only talking to him yesterday and he was tearing his hair out because the wire he'd ordered had been delayed.'

'I wouldn't worry too much about it——'

'Just a moment ago you said you were happy you were not in Jim's shoes!'

'Maybe,' Mrs Tibbs conceded with a lurking grin, 'but I'm not—yet, anyway, and if I were you I'd just let the boss be the boss. He's pretty good at it.'

'He really can't do much wrong in your eyes, can he?'

'Not a lot. Can't see much he's done wrong by you either so——'

But Sarah said tersely, 'We've been through this once before today, Mrs Tibbs; I think we should give it a rest.'

'Please yourself, Sarah.'

Sarah swung on her heel and departed in the direction of the study where things had gone ominously quiet. And as she entered it was to see Cliff standing in front of the window with his back to her and every line of his body was taut and curiously brooding. But that was nothing to what she saw as he wheeled about upon hearing someone come in. In fact she got such a shock at the blaze in his eyes and the lines stamped on his face, she took an uncertain breath and froze.

But that didn't stop her from seeing the effort he then made to banish it all, or the way he rubbed a hand to his brow briefly before he smiled and said, 'How are you?' and held out his hand to her.

'F-fine,' she stammered, still standing in the same spot.

'I suppose you heard me doing my nut and you've come to investigate. The thing is that before I landed I flew over all the fence lines that should have been repaired and they're still not done.'

'I know,' Sarah said cautiously. 'Jim told me but apparently the wire has been delayed.'

'Then he should have cancelled the order and gone to someone else,' Cliff said shortly before taking another visible grip on himself. 'Sarah——' his eyes suddenly had that wicked little look in them '—I'm not going to bite *you*.'

So she crossed the room slowly but the phone rang and he grimaced and she said with a faint smile, 'I'll leave you to it. Dinner should be ready in half an hour.'

But as she changed for dinner she found herself
thinking that it was not like Cliff to be unreasonable,
as she was pretty sure he had been over the fences,
and to wonder what else could have precipitated his
anger. She also, as she remembered the look in his
eyes, shivered slightly and felt a feather of...what
was it? she mused...touch her. Familiarity? But why?
He'd never been that angry with her.

Then, over dinner, Mrs Tibbs returned to the attack,
as if life weren't complicated enough.

She said as she served one of her famous curries,
'Actually got your wife to lie down after lunch today,
Cliff.'

'Well done, Mrs Tibbs!'

'Thought you'd appreciate it.'

'Thank you, Mrs Tibbs,' Sarah said drily. 'Please
don't bother to wait on us; we can manage.'

'Oh, I'm going, Sarah!' And she breezed out.

'What was that all about?' Cliff queried. 'Have you
two been fighting?'

Sarah opened her mouth to deny it but changed her
mind and said, 'I am a bit annoyed.'

'Why?'

'Because I sometimes feel as if I'm living in a
goldfish bowl,' she said tartly, still smarting from her
several run-ins with her housekeeper.

'It's never seemed to bother you before.'

'I lived a pretty simple life before...well...until...'
She stopped suddenly.

'Until I complicated things for you?' he suggested
with irony.

Sarah looked away and sighed suddenly. 'Cliff,
you've been wonderful—I don't know how to thank

you and I'm sorry I—well——' she lifted a hand '—you probably know what I mean.'

'Sarah,' he said slowly, 'it was my child too.'

Her eyes jerked suddenly to his face and widened painfully.

'What I mean is,' he went on, frowning slightly, 'there's nothing wonderful about trying to share this with you; it happened to *us*, I'm part of it and although I can never share the physical experience of it I can certainly try to ease your emotional burden— only...' he paused '...I'm not quite sure of the full extent of it.'

'What do you mean?' she asked after an aching little pause.

'I mean that I need you to tell me if there's more to this than I—can fathom.'

'No,' she said swiftly. 'No. They did tell me I would feel...unsettled for a while, though.'

'Yes.' He watched the way she clasped and unclasped her hands then lifted those penetrating dark eyes to hers again. 'But you're not still blaming yourself for it, are you? You never did explain why you said that.'

'I...I don't *know* why I said it,' she stammered. 'Perhaps it's only natural to wonder if there's something you could have done to prevent it—I think it must have been that.'

He narrowed his eyes thoughtfully but in the end all he said was, 'OK. Look, if it's going to be too much to have Amy and everyone around I can cancel them.'

'No!' she protested. 'Christmas is only a week away anyway—oh, no, I'm fine.'

And from the very next morning she set out to prove to all interested parties how fine she was.

Her sister-in-law and family arrived on Christmas Eve and there were decorations up and a beautifully trimmed tree in the lounge with tantalising presents set around its base—some of which Sarah had made, some she'd ordered by catalogue.

Amy added a load of presents herself and Sally and Ben speculated excitedly but were banned from touching before they scampered off to meet all their old friends.

And it was, Sarah thought, a happy family that joined all the employees and their families under the peppercorn trees in front of the machinery shed for a carols by candlelight session and Father Christmas's appearance, which was a long-cherished tradition on Edgeleigh.

She looked around and discovered that even she, who knew she was not happy despite the brave front she was putting on, who sometimes wondered if she'd ever be happy again, was lulled and soothed by the sight of candlelit faces, by the sight of Billy Pascoe firmly attaching himself to Darby Miller, the new teacher, with all the appearance of a hero-worshipper and not making one reference to Father Christmas's being Jim Lawson, in fact, and arriving on a horse instead of a reindeer sled. Soothed by the sight of Cindy Lawson, hand in hand with her new husband, and Donald Lawson, home for the holidays and full of a new confidence and maturity. Touched by the sight of Charlie, the tracker, who'd found her the day she'd sprained her ankle, singing Christmas carols with gusto and delight, and Mrs Tibbs with Sally on her ample lap. And finally Cliff, leaning against a tree looking relaxed but so obviously the pivot upon which Edgeleigh turned.

And she thought suddenly, I'm wrong not to make the best of this. I love them all, I love the life—why should I torture myself because Cliff can't give me his whole heart? Why can't I rid myself of the feeling that because I lost his child the reason I decided to go on with him is no longer there? *He* hasn't even seemed to consider it. Why can't I simply take Mrs Tibbs' words of wisdom to heart and believe that he's really done with Wendy Wilson except, perhaps, in the innermost reaches of his soul? The secret place where she can still set him on fire—do I believe that? I might not if I hadn't . . . felt the current go through his body that night at the Mirage, or heard him say what he did about peace and sanity and companionship. But I've either got to accept it now or . . .

'Sarah! Look what Father Christmas brought me!'

It was Ben flourishing a toy truck at her and shortly she was besieged by all her old pupils.

'We must be mad,' Amy said feelingly the next day at lunchtime.

It was hot and bright and they'd just consumed a vast hot meal of roast turkey and ham and Christmas pudding.

'Every year,' Amy continued, 'I make a vow that *next* year it will be salads and so on.'

'And every year you change your mind and say it won't be the same without a traditional Christmas dinner in the middle of the day,' Ross teased her.

'Well, I don't know about you lot——' Cliff reached for Sarah's hand '—but my wife and I are about to do the only sensible thing—take a siesta.'

'Bravo!' Ross and Amy chorused, and looked at each other.

'Not a bad idea, was it?'

The main bedroom was dark and cool and Sarah lay in Cliff's arms. They were only covered by a sheet and the overhead fan turned slowly above them. She'd changed into a nightshirt because he'd said that if they were going to do this they might as well do it properly. He'd simply peeled off all his clothes.

'No,' she said quietly, feeling full of food and wine and drowsy with it but with something still on her mind. 'Cliff——'

'I know,' he said wryly. 'We've still got a week or so to go before you get the all-clear to resume relations with me. Intimate relations, that is. I can wait.'

She relaxed. And presently she fell asleep in his arms so was not to know that it took him a while longer to do so and that although his words had been wry his eyes had been curiously sombre.

What she did know over the next days, however, was that the day when she was to go back to the base hospital for the check-up that would most probably give her that all-clear he'd mentioned was rushing towards her like a runaway train. I've got to have made up my mind *before* then, she told herself. I've got to have squared myself somehow to going on with him, because if I *can't* do it I must leave before I ever let him make love to me again.

Then something happened that made the decision for her, something so innocent yet so telling.

Ben got out a bundle of paintings he'd brought from Coorilla to show her, which he'd forgotten about in the excitement of Christmas.

'See, Sarah,' he said seriously as he lay on his tummy on the floor, his feet in the air and his chin on his hands and she sat beside him wading through sheets of butcher's paper covered with his art, 'I haven't forgotten what you taught me.'

'I can see that, Ben. These are really very good—you're doing your people much better,' she said of the stick-like figures that all the same did have a sense of movement about them. 'And I see you're being professional about it too.' She put her finger on his childish scrawl that was his signature. 'Who's this?'

'That's Uncle Cliff and Aunty Wendy. They stayed at Coorilla a couple of weeks ago,' he said vaguely. 'See, there's Sally and that's Robbo the dog and Uncle Cliff is throwing sticks for him. I was there with them but I didn't paint myself in. And this one——' he pushed another into Sarah's hand '—is Mum and Dad arguing, but not really mad like, just——' he screwed up his eyes '—a bit of a tiff. They don't fight like mad any more.'

'That's great, Ben,' Sarah said and hoped her voice sounded normal because she certainly didn't feel normal as everything fell into place—the day Cliff had come home from a night at Coorilla and been so disturbed. The feeling she'd had that there had to be more to it than some unfinished fences, the look in his eyes—and all of a sudden she remembered when she'd seen that look before. The night at the Sheraton Mirage when he'd seen Wendy and nearly crushed her hand almost as if he'd forgotten its very existence in his own.

'Sarah—you're not listening to me!'

'Sorry, Ben,' she murmured. 'OK, who's this . . . ?'

'Cliff, would you mind if I went for my check-up a day early?'

'Why? Is something wrong?' He searched her face narrowly.

'No,' she said casually. 'But the day it was booked for is Billy Pascoe's birthday, I've suddenly remembered. He's having a party and since he's such a reformed child...' She gestured.

He frowned. 'There's one problem. The day *before* your check-up is due is the day the parliamentary committee for flood relief is visiting the place.'

'Oh. So it is.' She chewed her lip. 'But do they want to see me?'

'No, but they certainly want to see me.'

'Well, could someone else fly me down? There's no need for you to be there. And I really am feeling fine so I'm sure there won't be any complications.'

'I suppose so,' he said with a frown. 'That's only the day after tomorrow.'

'Yes—it was just a thought,' she said and turned away.

'And it's just that I would rather be there with you,' he said. 'However——' and he put his hands on her shoulders and turned her back to face him '—in view of your well-known dedication to your pupils, go ahead.'

She smiled up at him and hoped her heartbreak wasn't showing in her eyes. 'Thanks.'

CHAPTER NINE

IT WAS so simple, Sarah was tempted to pinch herself.

She was flown to the big country town, she kept her remade appointment at the base hospital, was told she'd recovered completely from the miscarriage and the curette she'd had. She went back to the airport and told the helicopter pilot, who'd only started work recently on Edgeleigh, that she'd met up with some friends and decided to say a night with them, and gave him a letter for Cliff. She then put herself on a coach bound for Sydney but in fact changed coaches a couple of times and finally flew into Melbourne.

But it was feeling dazed, weary and heartsick that she rang the bell of a Toorak mansion and was admitted to Lady Pamela Sutherland's presence—her stepmother.

'My dear Sarah, this is a surprise,' Lady Pamela said, actually looking surprised, which was not something that happened to her often. 'I quite thought you'd intended to cut yourself off from me forever!'

Sarah sat down wearily in a gold, brocade-covered chair in a white and gold sitting-room and observed her ravishing, even though she was now past forty, golden-haired stepmother ironically. 'This is my home, Pam,' she said.

Pam grimaced. 'You don't need to rub it in. Your father did enough of that before he died.'

160

Sarah thought of her quiet, distinguished father who'd been an eminent banker and knighted for his services to the industry, and the sheer hell this woman had put him through but she sighed suddenly and thought, Then again, we all make mistakes, don't we? He didn't have to marry her in the first place, as I should never have married a man who, however much he may hate it, can still be set alight by another woman. 'I've always told you you're welcome to live here, Pam. That's not going to change. But I'll be here myself for a while, I'm not sure how long so——'

'Sarah!' Pam Sutherland got up and came over to her, her eyes riveted on Sarah's wedding-ring—she'd left the pearl and diamond engagement ring at Edgeleigh. 'Don't tell me you've gone and got yourself married! Darling . . . I'm speechless.' She then proceeded to demonstrate that she was no such thing. 'Where is he? Will *he* want to chuck me out? Oh, my God, don't tell me you did the one thing your father was afraid of—get married for your money?'

Sarah smiled. 'No. For my sanity, my companionship——' She broke off and had to take a deep breath. Then she thought, Let's get it over and done with . . . 'The thing is, Pam, I'm about to get myself unmarried. That's why I'm here. It's faintly possible I might need some support.'

'So you're afraid he's going to try to get his hands on half of what you've got? *Sarah*!'

Sarah got up, pushed past her stepmother impatiently and said angrily, 'Pam, for once in your life could you just stop thinking about *money*? No, he's not. He's got plenty of his own.'

'Then I don't understand . . .'

'You don't have to. All you have to do is arrange things with the staff so that I'm never at home to a Cliff Wyatt, or anyone without an appointment, for that matter. But even that won't be likely until the separation papers are served—he doesn't know who I am or where I come from.'

'Well, now I am speechless,' Pam Sutherland said and tottered back to her chair.

'And I'm exhausted,' Sarah said. 'I feel as if I could sleep for a week.'

She didn't. In fact she had difficulty sleeping that night in her old bedroom that was at the top of the house and had a sitting-room attached and was all tastefully and luxuriously furnished—her stepmother was an enthusiastic decorator but you couldn't deny she had taste. All her clothes were still in her dressing-room, neatly and carefully stored, and her books, early craft projects and desk in the sitting-room were dusted and just as she'd left them.

In fact the only thing that's changed is me, she mused painfully as she lay hopelessly wide awake in her ultra-comfortable bed. Gone forever is the bookish girl that was Sarah Sutherland, who studied so diligently for her degree here, took her first teaching jobs so seriously from here, and never knew the exquisite pleasure and pain of loving a man. Had never crumbled at a touch, ached with a need so strong it was a revelation, mourned for an unborn child too late—and burned in a private little hell because of what just the sight of another woman could do . . . Yes, who would have thought it of me? she reflected

and clenched her hands on the covers to stop herself
thinking about Cliff.

She dressed carefully the next morning in a timelessly
elegant cream linen suit with a mint-green silk blouse
and matching suede shoes, pinned her hair up in a
neat roll and went down for breakfast.

'I knew all those clothes I chose for you would get
used one day!' Pam, who was up uncharacteristically
early, said triumphantly. 'Where are you going?'

'To see the family solicitors,' Sarah answered, and
thanked the maid who poured her coffee. She didn't
recognise her but hadn't expected to. Her stepmother
had always had an uneasy relationship with domestic
staff—which was putting it kindly, actually, for she
was often a tyrant, often boringly petulant, so they
never stayed for long.

'Sarah, are you very sure . . . I mean, wouldn't you
at least like to *tell* me a bit more about it before you
do anything rash? Don't forget I've known you since
you were about twelve—God, that makes me feel old,'
she muttered, but recovered to say, 'And I know that
there are times when you can be as stubborn as a mule
and not always right!'

Sarah had to smile faintly as she recalled some of
the rebellious and, she had to admit, occasionally ridiculous stands she'd taken against her stepmother in
the early days. 'But that *was* when I was only twelve,
Pam,' she murmured.

Her stepmother snorted. 'You've got a short
memory—what about our last row? Before you took
yourself off into the wide blue yonder?'

Sarah subjected her to a clear blue gaze. 'You don't think I was entitled to object to tripping over your toyboys every time I came home, Pam?' she said gently.

'Sarah, I was going through a painful time,' Pam said with dignity. 'I was feeling old and—unloved. Unfortunately...' she hesitated '...I did discover that some of them made me feel...even older and less loved, so that period of my life is over now, but, be that as it may, I could have done with some support from you.'

Sarah looked at her, opened her mouth, closed it then said, 'I'm sorry. I'm glad to hear it. Is there—anyone?'

Pam's beautiful eyes flickered. 'There may be. He's proving a bit elusive but...' She shrugged and for once looked genuinely sad and every bit of her age.

And Sarah discovered a strange thing—she could no longer hate this woman or even despise her as much as she always had, and she wondered if it had anything to do with discovering her own human frailties. But she left the house not long afterwards and, although she remained resolute, spent a sad, disheartening day, but then she hadn't expected it to be any different.

What she also hadn't expected when she got home was to hear Cliff's voice coming from the gold and white sitting-room as she reached the top of the staircase.

She stopped, clutched the banister and wondered if she was hallucinating, but then it was too late. The door was open, she was visible through it and Pam sprang up and came towards her talking nineteen to the dozen...

'Don't be cross with me, please; I forgot to tell you it's the maid's afternoon off and I was totally unprepared when I answered the door—you *said* he didn't know, that he wouldn't come yet, but anyway, darling, are you *sure* you're doing the right thing? Personally——'

'Lady Sutherland...' Cliff loomed up behind her and for a moment Sarah's gaze clashed with his then he turned his attention back to Pam. '... I'll take the blame for this. Would you mind if I had some time alone with Sarah?'

'No! No! I'll go—Sarah, don't look like that, please. You've no idea,' she said agitatedly, 'how stubborn she can be, Mr Wyatt, but I'll... go.' And she walked away.

'How did you find me so quickly?' Sarah said tonelessly as soon as the sitting-room door was firmly closed.

'I always knew who you were.'

She turned slowly to face him across the room. He looked unfamiliar in a dark suit and tie, unfamiliar but devastatingly attractive and entirely at home in Pam's sitting-room—and she couldn't blame Pam for reeling—something inside *her* was reeling and spinning, but she knew she couldn't allow it to go on, and she couldn't allow herself to be intimidated by the lack of expression in his eyes, the set lines beside his mouth that to her now indicated that he was going to fight and fight in that diabolical way he had that was so hard to answer.

'*Always*?' she said.

'From long before we got married—I told you you intrigued me, Sarah. It wasn't hard to make some enquiries.'

'But the only address I ever gave was my solicitors' and they wouldn't have given any information out about me without my consent.'

'I guessed as much—which prompted some further curiosity on my part so I consulted the Department of Education. It was easy from there on. One wonders,' he murmured and raised a mocking eyebrow at her, 'why you were so determined to keep it all from me. Did you honestly believe I might turn out to be a fortune-hunter, Sarah?'

'One could also wonder why you never told me you knew,' she said stiffly.

'Well, I *can* tell you that—I decided two could play that game and if you liked to have an extra string to your bow, so to speak, then I would do the same. In case you ever took it into your head to do a bunk— just as you did do, in fact,' he finished softly but with a rapier-like glance that cut her to the quick. 'You don't think you could have done better than make use of Billy Pascoe and his birthday party—such a re-formed kid, incidentally? I feel that was rather a— poor shot.'

She coloured and trembled and his dark, arrogant gaze saw it all as it roamed her elegant outfit. But she lifted her chin and said coldly, 'If I could ever talk reason to you, Cliff, I wouldn't have to resort to——'

'Lies and trickery?' he suggested gently.

'Whatever. But I knew you wouldn't listen to me; I knew you'd . . . overwhelm me——'

'Once I was able to make love to you again? Why the hell do you think I can do that, Sarah?' he said in a different, harder voice. 'Don't you think it might have something to do with how much you love me?'

She went white but she also got angry. 'Cliff, you can taunt me with that as much as you like but it's also one reason why I *can't* go on being your safe harbour from Wendy Wilson. I can't continue to provide your physical release, your peace and your sanity, because to me it's like living on a volcano. Do you think I didn't realise that the night at the Mirage; do you think if I hadn't been pregnant I wouldn't have gone then? Do you think I don't know that it's happened since?'

'What do you mean?' he shot at her.

She gestured. 'The night you came home from Coorilla and were so angry—it wasn't about fences, was it?'

He stared at her for a long moment then said roughly, 'Bloody Amy again——'

'No. It wasn't; it was just——'

'Then who?' he ground out.

'It doesn't matter but it *wasn't* Amy—and it's true, isn't it? You were with Wendy. Look, Cliff, what I'm trying to say is, whether it's to love or hate or both, she *moves* you as I never will. And if I'd stayed all I could see was...myself turning sour and bitter, even starting to look for it, getting jealous over imaginary things and...' She stopped and sighed. 'I can't do it, and nothing you can say will make me change my mind. I...already have the evidence of how it...affects me. And there's one thing I have to tell you: I rarely take advantage of or even appreciate what my father left me, but this is one occasion when I'll use all the considerable resources I have to hand to—end this marriage.'

'Sarah, if I tell you that I never for one moment regretted marrying you and that all *she* moves me to is disgust and fury because of her tactics, her ethics, her...and I wasn't *with* her incidentally; I had no idea she'd be there——'

'It doesn't matter; I wouldn't believe you, Cliff,' she said steadily and walked to the door. 'If you wouldn't mind having my things sent here, I'd be grateful. And you'll be hearing from my solicitors shortly.'

'So...' he didn't move an inch but his eyes were more shockingly insolent and mocking than she'd ever seen them '...whatever came afterwards—the way you slept with me, the way I slept with you, the life we led and shared and loved—are you telling me that none of that could ever remove the stigma in your mind of seeing me kiss another woman? Are you telling me none of it persuaded you that I'd come to love you—however I may have gone into our marriage?'

'No, I do think you love me in a way, Cliff. It's just not the right way for me. And, as I've tried to tell you before, this could all be more my fault than yours. I didn't—know myself really. But I do now.'

There was a long, taut silence then he said, his eyes suddenly unreadable, 'What will you do?'

'I don't know. I haven't thought too much about it yet. Something will come up.'

'What about your passion for teaching?'

'I, well—perhaps. What will——?' She stopped abruptly.

'I do?' He lifted an eyebrow. 'Go back to being a bachelor—until, that is, I can find another impressionable virgin to persuade to share my bed with a view to marrying me so that she can take care of my physical needs, my need for peace, sanity and companionship while I yearn for another woman— what else? Only this time I'd better make sure she isn't Sir Paul Sutherland's daughter in disguise with such resources——'

'Cliff, they were your *own* words,' she cried, then stopped and bit her lip.

'Some of them,' he conceded. 'And those that were, such as peace and companionship, were things we found together, Sarah, in a way that I'll be surprised if we ever find them again with anyone else. But I never slept with you for any other reason than because I wanted *you*, not someone to fulfil my physical needs, as you rather primly put it, while I was burning for another woman—as you no doubt thought rather colourfully but didn't quite say. But I've got the feeling I could say this until the cows come home; I could even make love to you the way you love it, the way you revel in it, until they come home too but you wouldn't believe it. So I guess this is goodbye. There is one other thing, though. If this is the after-effect of your miscarriage——'

'It's not,' she whispered. 'I'm fine. Will you please see yourself out?' And she fled to the safety of her bedroom.

She refused to see him the next day when he came again or to have any communication with him through her solicitor. Then all such efforts ceased abruptly.

'Sarah—I'm so worried about you!' Pam said two weeks later. 'Please let me call a doctor. You won't talk about it, you're hardly eating, you look terrible—if being away from Cliff Wyatt affects you so much, *why*——?'

'No, it's over now, Pam,' Sarah said with resolution. 'I've decided to go away for a bit of a holiday—would you like to come?'

Shock nearly caused Pam to choke. 'Me? Why? Where? The seaside? Or some lovely tropical island?'

'Not the seaside as in Surfer's or the Gold Coast,' Sarah said definitely. 'And I think tropical islands at this time of the year are too hot and prone to cyclones anyway.' She frowned. 'I don't really know where I'd like to go, just somewhere quiet and not raining...' She grimaced and gestured towards the window where Melbourne's temperamental weather was behaving like the middle of winter instead of the middle of summer.

Pam sat up. 'Could you wait about ten days and would you...? No, you probably wouldn't.'

'Tell me.'

'You know Robert,' Pam said slowly.

Sarah nodded. She'd met the new man in Pam's life and been unwittingly impressed, even moved to wonder if her stepmother was turning over a new leaf.

'He's a mad golfer,' Pam continued a little gloomily, 'but I suppose it could be worse—anyway, he's suggested a week at a golfing resort. It's called Kooralbyn and it's just across the Queensland border from New

South Wales. Apparently there's a new, divine hotel on it with some marvellous restaurants; it's out in the country, miles from anywhere, yet it has wonderful facilities—a health club and beauty centre, tennis, horse-riding, *sky-diving* if you're into that kind of thing—but it's also peaceful and the scenery is magnificent as well as having one of the top golf courses in the country—why don't you come with us?'

Sarah's first reaction had been to think, Not Queensland, but then she thought that the New South Wales border was about six hundred miles from Edgeleigh, so... 'Robert might not appreciate having me along, though,' she said slowly.

'My dear,' Pam said honestly, 'you are one of the best things I've got going for me so far as Robert's concerned; he's very impressed. But he and I would be... sharing a room, would you mind that?'

Sarah smiled. 'Of course not. Well...'

'And you used to play golf with your father and love it!'

'I haven't played for years, though——'

'Oh, do it, darling!' Pam said excitedly. 'You do need a break and you do need company and even though it's ten days away we could plan our wardrobes in the meantime!'

Kooralbyn lived up to all expectations.

Set in a beautiful valley with Mount Lindesay as a spectacular backdrop, the countryside was grassy, studded with wonderful gum trees and dotted with ponds and dams. There were birds and ducks everywhere and in the late afternoons kangaroos emerged from the bush and grazed peacefully on the Par Three golf course in front of the hotel.

Sarah had a room facing the golf course and it was delightfully decorated and furnished with cottagey touches but all mod cons. And at night some of the huge trees were floodlight from the ground, creating a wonderful spectacle.

She put herself entirely in Pam and Robert's hands, which meant she spent a lot of time in the beauty and health centre as well as playing a lot of golf, and every evening she dressed up to satisfy Pam who loved dining at either Lilies or Kooka's, both very exclusive restaurants. But she did take herself for a solitary walk every day beneath the wide blue sky and it never failed to strike her that Kooralbyn had once been a great grazing property. Will I ever be able to wrench my thoughts away from...things like that? she wondered.

It was on her last day that she picked up a Queensland newspaper and was reading it desultorily after breakfast in the sunshine when her eyes fell on a small item with the heading 'Grazier Still Critical'. She read on with the peculiar sensation of all her blood draining to her feet. It said...

Prominent grazier, Cliff Wyatt, who was involved in a helicopter accident a week ago, is still in Intensive Care in a critical condition at the Royal Brisbane Hospital. Wyatt, 35, was a passenger in the helicopter that encountered a freak storm on a flight from his property, Edgeleigh, in Western Queensland. Both the pilot and the one other passenger escaped with minor injuries when the helicopter crashed. Mr Wyatt is married with no children...

'*Sarah*! What is it?'

Mutely Sarah offered the paper to Pam. And for once in her life Pam didn't say a word, she just sprang into action. Which was how, barely an hour later, Sarah, Pam and Robert were taxiing down the Kooralbyn airstrip in a light plane bound for Brisbane.

'I'm very sorry but only the immediate family are allowed to see Mr Wyatt——'

'She's his wife and I'm his mother-in-law,' Pam said to the sister, striking one of her haughty attitudes, and Sarah, even through her pain and misery, knew exactly what was to come. 'I'm also *Lady* Pamela Sutherland and——'

But it was unnecessary; the sister focused suddenly on Sarah and said, 'Mrs Wyatt? Please come with me. His sister is with him—I'll ask her to come out and have a word with you first.'

'Sarah?' Amy stumbled towards her no more than a minute later, her face white and anguished. 'Oh, where have you been? We had no idea where even to start looking...'

'I'm here now, Amy.' Sarah embraced the other girl. 'How...is he?'

'Not good. He's got a fractured skull, a collapsed lung, a broken leg, but he's so...restless when he's conscious. They say——'

The sister intervened. 'Let's just take Mrs Wyatt through, Mrs Collins—Doctor is with Mr Wyatt now.'

How she restrained herself from weeping when she saw Cliff lying so still, covered by a single sheet with his eyelids taped down, and hooked up to so many machines, she never knew. What she did know was that even looking so still, so thin, pale and unfamiliar, every one his features—the dark hair on his chest, his broad shoulders—all of it struck her with the almost unbearable knowledge that she loved him as she'd never loved anyone or ever would, yet she'd not been with him in this crisis.

'Cliff,' she whispered, bending over him. 'Oh, *Cliff*…what am I allowed to do?' she asked the doctor desperately.

'You can talk to him and touch him, Mrs Wyatt.' The sister had been conferring quietly with him. 'We have him sedated because as soon as we bring him out of it he gets particularly disturbed, which doesn't do his injuries any good—but he can probably hear you although he won't be able to respond at the moment. Sit down, take his hand or stroke his brow and try not to project an overwrought image of yourself, however hard that might be, Mrs Wyatt,' the doctor finished barely audibly.

She swallowed and called on every inner resource she had. 'Cliff? Cliff, it's me, Sarah. Remember me? You used to say I was a school-marm born and bred but actually if there was one thing I preferred to teaching it was being your wife…'

She talked for nearly two hours, gently, sometimes whimsically; she talked about Mrs Tibbs and Billy Pascoe and Cindy Lawson's wedding-dress. She talked about their life together at Edgeleigh, all the little anecdotes she remembered, anything she could think of. And all the while she held his hand or stroked his hair, and prayed inwardly.

Then finally the doctor said, 'This lot of sedation is due to wear off now, Mrs Wyatt. We're going to take a chance and see how he reacts without any further sedatives, whether he...well, we'll see.'

So she kept talking and they moved the tapes from his eyelids and she felt a slight movement in his hand then he opened his eyes, licked his dry, cracked lips and said, 'Sarah? Is it really you?'

'Yes, Cliff. I came back—forever, if you want me.'

'Thank God,' he said, and moved his hand so that it covered and held hers as if he would never let it go. And then he fell into a deep, peaceful sleep.

'It worked,' the doctor said with quiet triumph as he and two sisters monitored all the machines minutely. 'He's relaxed at last. I can't say we're entirely out of the woods yet, Mrs Wyatt, but it's going to be so much easier now that he's not fighting us all the time. You've wrought a small miracle.'

That was when Sarah at last allowed the tears to flow over.

CHAPTER TEN

IT WAS a month before Cliff was released from hospital and even then his leg was still in plaster and he had to use crutches. But he took a deep breath on the front steps of the hospital and said fervently, 'Hell— I never thought I'd get out of here.'

Sarah slipped her arm through his. 'I know how you must have felt but, Cliff, are you sure you want to go straight back to Edgeleigh?'

'Yes, Cliff, why don't you come to Coorilla at least?' Amy pleaded. 'We're much closer to Brisbane and you'll have to have check-ups——'

'No,' he said with a flickering smile. 'I'm going back to Edgeleigh today, I'm flying back in a chopper, I'm taking my wife with me—and that's all there is to it.'

It wasn't easy to get him into the new helicopter because of his leg but he was so determined, they made it somehow, then Sarah squeezed in beside him and they took off from Archerfield and she held his hand, and when she saw the sweat on his brow and the nerve beating in his jawline she laid her head on his shoulder and put her arm around his waist. He said nothing but slipped her hair rhythmically through his long fingers.

When they landed safely at Edgeleigh, she felt all his muscles relax and saw him swallow, and he spoke at last. 'It'll never be that hard again.'

'I think you deserve a medal.'

'Actually, I think you deserve a medal for putting up with me this last month—my moods, my impatience, the lot.'

But she only smiled a wise little smile into his eyes.

Of course there was a reception committee waiting for them. There was even a banner with 'WELCOME HOME BOSS' painted on it, and a party organised under the peppercorn trees. And no one said a word about how gaunt and thin he was although Sarah saw the shock of it in their eyes. And no one said a word about her mysterious disappearance, not even Mrs Tibbs after she'd broken the party up and ordered both Cliff and Sarah up to the homestead.

But I won't escape it forever, Sarah thought as Cliff stood on the veranda propped on his crutches and breathed deeply again. 'Come,' she said quietly. 'You need to rest now.'

'*You're* not going to treat me like a patient too, Sarah, I hope,' he said wryly.

'No. I'll let you up for dinner if you have a rest now.'

'If that's not——'

'You just do as you're told, Cliff Wyatt!' Mrs Tibbs said aggressively, which was her way of showing concern.

'All right! All right! I know when I'm beaten.' But in fact he did look exhausted.

'So you're back. To stay?'

'Yes, Mrs Tibbs.' They were in the kitchen drinking tea as the sun slipped beyond the horizon.

'He was like a man demented when you left.'

'Was he?'

'Uh-huh. Still, all's well that ends well; I guess you've sorted everything out between you now and I won't say any more on the subject.'

Sarah looked at her with surprise but affection in her eyes and said quietly, 'Thank you.'

'What's this I hear about you being the daughter of a lord, then?'

'I'm not—how on earth did you hear that anyway?'

'Well, you know what the bush telegraph is like— coulda sworn that's what it said, and I was all set to call you "milady"!'

'My father was a knight but it's my stepmother who is the Lady; it wasn't an inherited thing. You'll probably meet her.'

'That a fact? Never met one before—I'll look forward to it.' And she got up to attend to her dinner, leaving Sarah to chuckle inwardly and think, The mind boggles! But then she sobered as she thought of something else Mrs Tibbs had said, about her and Cliff's sorting things out between them, and wondered what Mrs Tibbs would say if she knew that they'd discussed nothing. But perhaps we'll never need to, she mused. Perhaps it was all said that first day in the intensive care unit...

And her mind roamed back over the past month. It had been two weeks before he'd even been capable of feeding himself or concentrating for any length of time so that by the time he could she'd grown so much part of his routine, it was as if they'd never been apart. And as he'd slowly grown stronger she'd exerted every nerve to make his stay in hospital as pleasant as possible. She'd read to him, played cards with him, watched television with him, spoken daily to Edgeleigh and also to Ross, who had taken over the reins of the empire, and filled him in on all that was happening. But he'd said nothing about her coming back and she'd followed suit as if it was all settled.

So why do I have the premonition it's not? she asked herself, staring unseeingly at her empty teacup. Then she glanced up at a sound and saw him standing in the doorway on his crutches looking rested but watching her intently.

She smiled and stood up. 'I hope you're hungry. Mrs Tibbs has prepared a feast!'

'Yes. I am. What were you thinking about, Sarah? You looked—about a million miles away.'

'Nothing. Would you like a little treat?'

He raised an eyebrow at her. 'Such as?'

'A drink before dinner?'

'I thought you were never going to ask...'

They went to bed early.

At least they retired to their bedroom early, but just as she was about to help him change he said, 'Sarah, could we talk for a while?'

Her hands stilled on the belt of his trousers that they'd had slit up one side-seam to get over his cast. 'If you like, Cliff, but——'

'Yes, I'd like, and I'm quite up to it,' he said gently, and, taking her hand, awkwardly manoeuvred them so that they could sit side by side on the bed. He laid his crutches aside and said, 'Because I'd very much like to know if you're doing all this, more than I could ever thank you for, out of pity.'

She caught her breath and whispered, 'No! Of course not, Cliff.'

'Then out of love?' he queried, taking her chin in his fingers and turning her face towards him.

'Yes . . .'

'But there was a time not so long ago when you hated loving me, Sarah, and I've done nothing, that you know about at least, to change the conditions that made you feel that way.'

'Cliff, don't.'

'Yes, Sarah.' He ran the tips of his fingers down her neck. 'I have to try to make you believe that once it really hit me that I'd lost you Wendy Wilson lost the last vestiges of whatever it was she held over me. She no longer has the power to move me at all—even that last time at Coorilla, what got to me was not *her* as such, I realised finally, or all the years of my life she wasted; it was that she still thought she was so much sexier, more desirable than you, so unforgettable, and had no idea she didn't even know the first thing about being a real woman like you.

'That's what moved me—you, not her—but like the idiot I was I still couldn't put it into words—until I lost you and finally began to know what I'd done. It took that to make me understand at last, to make me aware of how I'd allowed you to think . . . the things you did because I couldn't rid myself of her poison, because I couldn't let myself trust again. That's why I declared my love for you like a half-hearted fool; that's why I was so sure when I found you in Melbourne that I could win you back but didn't realise I was still only half committing myself.

'It was only,' he said slowly, 'when I got back to Edgeleigh that I sat down and really faced the prospect that you were determined not to come back. And that was when I couldn't get it out of my mind that you might never have wanted our child and that's what I'd done to you, and to us, by letting you think I didn't love you in the ultimate way. And that's when a kind of hell began for me that made Wendy... nothing.'

'Oh, Cliff,' she whispered with tears slipping down her cheeks. 'I deluded myself about that.' And she told him how she'd felt after she'd miscarried. 'That is why I left as much as any other reason. When I was losing it, I knew I wanted your child more than anything else, that it didn't matter to me if I couldn't have all of your heart, but, you see, I'd made myself believe it did.'

He drew an unsteady breath. 'And that's what you meant when you said you'd deserved to lose it? Sarah... oh, God, don't believe that; it had nothing to do with it.'

'I know, I know, but, you see, I hadn't even let myself think about it when I had it—that's the kind of mess I'd got myself into and that's what I meant when I said I hadn't known myself properly, known that I was capable of that kind of self-deception or that kind of... jealousy.'

'Yet you were prepared to take me on again—even though I *caused* all that?' he said intensely, wiping her tears away with his fingers. 'Sarah, that's what I was afraid of—pity.'

She kissed his fingers. 'Not pity, Cliff. Just sudden, heartbreaking sanity. Just the bare facts—that I *loved* you as I would never love anyone else, and that if you died I would never be properly alive again.'

He said something under his breath then swept her into his arms. 'I feel the same; I just wish I could prove it to you,' he said torturedly.

'You did,' she whispered. 'I don't think anyone's told you this, how close you were—to the brink, but it was *me* you came back for...' She smiled through her tears. 'And you never did send my things back.'

He woke in the middle of the night, cursed his cast as it impeded him and felt for her immediately. And she felt his heart beating heavily as he pulled her nightgown away and kissed her breasts with a sort of desperation.

'Cliff, it's all right, I'm here—are you awake?'

She felt him relax slowly then he said with a smile in his voice, 'I don't know why you keep accusing me of doing this in my sleep.'

She stroked his hair. 'I thought you were having a nightmare.'

'I was. I used to get them regularly in hospital—didn't the sister tell you?'

Sarah's lips curved into a smile. 'No, but the doctor did tell me we should take this kind of thing slowly.'

'He didn't say a word to me about it.'

'Perhaps he thought he—might be wasting his time.'

'I suspect he might have. So the burden of being sane and sensible about it rests squarely with you, Mrs Wyatt, as ever.'

'Yes, well,' Sarah said slowly and drew her hands down his chest, 'I don't know where everyone gets this "sensible" picture of me from.'

'Nor, now, do I,' Cliff said with a catch in his voice. 'Sarah...'

'Hush, I'm in charge for once—and you're the one with your leg in a plaster cast so you'll just have to...put up with this.'

He groaned. 'Put up with it! I'm liable to die from it; it's exquisite.'

'Good,' she said with a certain amount of satisfaction in her voice which caused him to laugh softly.

But later, when she was lying against his side with his arm around her and their breathing had returned to normal, he said in a deep, quiet voice, 'I love you, Sarah. I think I started to love you when you first blinked at me from behind your glasses and then offered to punch me in the mouth. I love your petiteness, your huge spirit...so many things. But most of all I love the way you make love to me. It—I don't know but it's like a revelation every time.'

'It is for me too. Cliff?' She put her hand to his cheek then said, 'Nothing.'

'Tell me,' he prompted.

'I was going to say something trite and silly about how we've forged ourselves through so much that it has to be so much stronger now, what we feel.'

'Not trite and very true.' He kissed the top of her head. 'When do you think you might have first fallen in love with me?'

She smiled. 'Well, if you really want to know, you knocked me for six that first day as well—but I think you always did know.'

'I would have had to be a supreme optimist to imagine I did anything but fill you with disgust,' he said wryly. 'Go on.'

'If you're not going to admit you were very well aware I was...a bit knocked for six, no, I won't,' Sarah teased.

'I was just trying to prove to you what a reformed person I am. All those caddish, not to mention unpleasantly macho male ways are behind me now, you see,' he said gravely.

'Want to bet?'

He buried his face in her neck and laughed softly. 'Talking of bets—we had another going once.'

'I remember it well,' she murmured.

'Ah—but are you going to respond?'

'You win. You're a lovely husband most of the time, actually. You...how can I put it? Oh, yes; do you remember once saying to me that what I lacked was moonlight and roses?'

'Yes. That was the first time I kissed you—well, took intolerable advantage of you,' he said wickedly.

'I knew you'd never reform completely, Cliff Wyatt. But——'

'Yes, miss?'

Her lips trembled. 'I'd love to be able to tell you otherwise at the moment,' she said severely, 'but your brand of moonlight and roses makes me feel like the luckiest woman alive.'

She'd thought he'd continue in the same light-hearted vein but his hands tightened on her almost unbearably for a moment, causing her to say urgently, 'Cliff, are you all right? Has——?'

'No, I'm not all right,' he answered in a strained voice quite unlike his usual one, 'but not because I'm sick. I'm thinking that I don't deserve you but I love you so much, Sarah, yet all I can do is . . . joke about it.'

'Oh, Cliff,' she whispered, moving in his arms and feeling the tension in his body, even a dew of sweat on his brow as she put her hand to it soothingly. 'Cliff, I love *you*, please believe me—what can I do to show you?'

'Stay with me forever, Sarah.'

'I will,' she vowed.

Two weeks later, Sarah rose from the breakfast table hurriedly and returned in ten minutes looking pale and flustered, causing Mrs Tibbs, who was clearing dishes away, to say, 'Now just sit down, Sarah, and try a piece of dry toast and a cup of black tea.' She also went on to marvel, 'It's *amazing* what some people can do with a plaster cast on!'

Cliff, still drinking his coffee, grinned but said modestly, 'I can't take all the credit for it, I'm afraid, Mrs Tibbs, much as I'd love to.'

'I should think not! Let's see . . .' And she started to count on her fingers.

'When you two have quite finished . . .' Sarah said, but Cliff put his hand over hers and murmured,

'Happy?'

'Oh, *yes*,' she said.

And, about eight and a half months later, she was safely delivered of a boy who weighed in at seven pounds and caused his father to say with deep satisfaction, 'I think he looks a bit like—us.'

'Do you really? Be a bit strange if he didn't,' his mother replied.

'What I mean is, he's got my colouring but there's something about him that's a lot like you.'

And Sarah, watching the fascination in Cliff's eyes as he gazed down at his son, wiped a sudden tear away. 'Anyway, so long as you like him.'

He turned his dark gaze to her. 'You do realise why, don't you?'

'You could always tell me,' she said softly.

'Well, it's all to do with my ongoing love-affair with his mother.' And he put his arms around her.

Sarah leant against him and felt his warmth and strength surround her. Her lips curved into a smile and she laid her cheek against his. 'I love you too...'

anniversary
Temptation
is Ten!

Join the festivities as Mills & Boon celebrates Temptation's tenth anniversary in February 1995.

There's a whole host of in-book competitions and special offers with some great prizes to be won—watch this space for more details!

In March, we have a sizzling new mini-series Lost Loves about love lost...love found. And, of course, the Temptation range continues to offer you fun, sensual exciting stories all year round.

After ten tempting years, nobody can resist

Temptation
anniversary

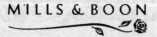

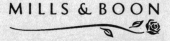

Next Month's Romances

Each month you can choose from a wide variety of romance with Mills & Boon. Below are the new titles to look out for next month, why not ask either Mills & Boon Reader Service or your Newsagent to reserve you a copy of the titles you want to buy – just tick the titles you would like and either post to Reader Service or take it to any Newsagent and ask them to order your books.

Please save me the following titles:	Please tick	✓
BURNING WITH PASSION	Emma Darcy	
THE WRONG KIND OF WIFE	Roberta Leigh	
RAW SILK	Anne Mather	
ONE NIGHT OF LOVE	Sally Wentworth	
THUNDER ON THE REEF	Sara Craven	
INVITATION TO LOVE	Leigh Michaels	
VENGEFUL BRIDE	Rosalie Ash	
DARK OASIS	Helen Brooks	
YESTERDAY'S HUSBAND	Angela Devine	
TAINTED LOVE	Alison Fraser	
NO PLACE FOR LOVE	Susanne McCarthy	
THAT DEVIL LOVE	Lee Wilkinson	
SHINING THROUGH	Barbara McMahon	
MANDATE FOR MARRIAGE	Catherine O'Connor	
DESERT MAGIC	Mons Daveson	
DANGEROUS FLIRTATION	Liz Fielding	

If you would like to order these books in addition to your regular subscription from Mills & Boon Reader Service please send £1.90 per title to: Mills & Boon Reader Service, Freepost, P.O. Box 236, Croydon, Surrey, CR9 9EL, quote your Subscriber No:................................. (if applicable) and complete the name and address details below. Alternatively, these books are available from many local Newsagents including W H Smith, J Menzies, Martins and other paperback stockists from 10 February 1995.

Name:...

Address:...

.............................Post Code:.........................

To Retailer: If you would like to stock M&B books please contact your regular book/magazine wholesaler for details.

You may be mailed with offers from other reputable companies as a result of this application. If you would rather not take advantage of these opportunities please tick box. ☐

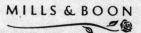

GET 4 BOOKS
AND A MYSTERY GIFT

Return the coupon below and we'll send you 4 Mills & Boon romances absolutely FREE! We'll even pay the postage and packing for you.

We're making you this offer to introduce you to the benefits of Reader Service: FREE home delivery of brand-new Mills & Boon romances, at least a month before they are available in the shops, FREE gifts and a monthly Newsletter packed with information.

Accepting these FREE books places you under no obligation to buy, you may cancel at any time, even after receiving just your free shipment. Simply complete the coupon below and send it to:

HARLEQUIN MILLS & BOON, **FREEPOST**, PO BOX 70, CROYDON CR9 9EL.

- -

Yes, please send me 4 Mills & Boon romances and a mystery gift as explained above. Please also reserve a subscription for me. If I decide to subscribe I shall receive 6 superb new titles every month for just £11.40* postage and packing free. I understand that I am under no obligation whatsoever. I may cancel or suspend my subscription at any time simply by writing to you, but the free books and gift will be mine to keep in any case.
I am over 18 years of age.

1EP5R

Ms/Mrs/Miss/Mr _____

Address _____

_____

_____

_____ Postcode _____